WHAT IT COST US

Shout Mouse Press is a nonprofit writing and publishing program dedicated
to amplifying underheard youth voices. Learn more and see our full catalog
at www.shoutmousepress.org

Shout Mouse Press
1638 R Street NW, Suite 218
Washington, DC 20009

Trade distribution: Ingram Book Group

For information about special discounts and bulk purchases, please contact
Shout Mouse Press sales at 240-772-1545 or orders@shoutmousepress.org

WHAT IT COST US

STORIES OF PANDEMIC & PROTEST IN DC

by the Young Authors of Shout Mouse Press

For young people like us:
That you may find your own way
to pick up the pieces
of what you've faced.
There's always a way forward.
Keep going.

CONTENTS

SPRING

The Storm, the Rainbow, and Valentina

Not What I Signed Up For

A Ramadan to Remember

SUMMER

FALL

WINTER

FOREWORD

by Candice Iloh

Author of *Every Body Looking*
and *Break This House*

On Tuesday, September 22, 2020 we rose early. The living room was a sunlit mess of boxes, half-opened backpacks, and plastic bags stuffed with leftovers from last night's takeout. I'd walked out to the living room with my best friend's words echoing in my brain: *Just tell me the dates and I'ma be there*, she'd said a year ago. Now she was here, laid across my living room couch with her signed copy of my book rested at her side. Her face beamed like a celebrity had just entered the room, and an overly-dramatic slow clap began the minute I got to the end of the hallway. I stood there in my pajamas, bashful, crust still clustering the corners of my eyes.

We had a whole list of things to do before it was time. We needed to pick up my medication from the store. We needed to order breakfast. I needed to cut my hair. We needed to go outside and stage the most epic photoshoot possible against the yellow wall that I'd scouted just weeks before. I needed to post photos to Instagram to let the world know that I'd finally done it. It was the day my debut novel, *Every Body Looking*, had finally entered the world and that night would be the official launch… on Zoom.

I'd been dreaming of this moment for over ten years. I'd dreamt about the kinds of questions I would be asked by the audience. Imagined the chapter I'd read to them from the stage. Had practiced things I wanted to say about all the hell I'd gone through to push this debut novel out into the world. And for months just before the first COVID-19 death had been announced, I could even feel the humidity against my skin in the crowded bookstore that would host this highly anticipated arrival. But none of that happened. None of that was ever going to happen. I was going to introduce my first book to an audience that I couldn't see nor hear from my computer screen where I could only interact with the facial expressions of the host alongside my own. There would be no physical audience to hug, shake hands with, or sign books for when the event ended. That night I closed my laptop to the silence of an empty bedroom under the glow of an expensive ring light, trying to keep up with what everyone called the new normal.

No matter how hard my best friend had worked that day to make the moment feel special. No matter the work she put in to record the hours leading up to the launch as I danced, got dressed, and reflected on what the day meant to me, I couldn't shake the almost-debilitating grief that haunted the whole day. I couldn't pretend like this was what I wanted or planned. It didn't feel fair that I could never have another debut release again. After all, debut means *first*. And, in this case, it also meant *last*. There would be no do-overs and I would have to accept that all my sacrifice for this dream still felt like an incredible loss.

As a writer I could boastfully say I know loss like the back of my hand. I might even go as far as telling someone that it comes with "the job." That, to be an artist of any kind is to know, intimately, what it is like to have things slip through the cracks at any point in the process. To be rejected from the only thing you've ever lived for. Whether it be to the things you created, now released into the world, or to the things you once imagined happening a specific way; to dreams remixed. We writers are supposed to learn to let go of an expectation like it is nothing. Like some sort of rite of passage. Everything must change. Everything must end. Everything must go. Everything must die. That's... just the way it is. In ways, 2020 felt like the world was finally getting a taste of the artist life. Canceled this. Loss of wages that. Things coming to an unexplained halt that we all had to deal with.

But we writers are also human. And if you are anything like the next person, saying goodbye might take you some practice. Might take you multiple attempts before you fully build the muscle that makes you sturdy enough to accept a thing passing and how that exact moment in time will never exist again. The sweetness of a blip in time that we've worked long and hard to experience. A blip that arrives and leaves quicker than we could have ever expected. Feeling nothing like what it had been hyped up to be because no one could have seen this version of life coming.

These ten authors whose stories make *What It Cost Us* offer us the satisfaction of holding space for that emptiness. Those gaping holes where art imitates the heartbreak and sacrifice of this strange new life. Chronicled by the pandemic and political headlines of 2020 and the seasons of the American calendar, these writers reckon with young life amid a sudden shift into virtual school, social distancing, quarantine, and mass pandemonium while trying to hold onto the things that mean the most to us all.

In "A Ramadan to Remember," Iman Ilias writes:

> *It's so ironic how infrequently you realize you care about something until it's taken away from you. I would give anything to go back to those quiet afternoons, meditating on the mosque garden and anticipating the delicious food I would dig into at iftar time. Back then, that was a typical Ramadan day, nothing out of the ordinary. Now, it seems like such a gift.*

If you are reading this, you are still here and holding a collection of hope in your hands. Hands that feed you, write for you, and shift the weight around for you every day in your continued journey in this new terrain. Every day we navigate life after a collective cost that many of us are still paying but, here, we get to think about what it means to go on. What it means to change direction. What it means to try on the day again and again.

———————————————————————————————

Candice Iloh is a first-generation Nigerian American writer from the Midwest by way of Washington, DC and Brooklyn, New York whose books center home, self-awareness, and Black sustainability. They are a proud alumna of the Rhode Island Writers Colony and their work has earned fellowships from Lambda Literary, VONA, Kimbilio Fiction and a residency with Hi-ARTS, where they debuted their first one-person show in 2018. Candice became a 2020 National Book Award Finalist and in 2021, a Printz Award Honoree for their debut novel, Every Body Looking. Break This House *is their second novel.*

INTRODUCTION

by Alexa Patrick

Programs Director, Shout Mouse Press

In January of 2022, ten Shout Mouse alumni authors from various backgrounds — DC-native, immigrant, Latinx, Black, Muslim, and intersections thereof — gathered for the first time to write a collaborative book set in DC about the hardest year of our collective lives: 2020. And they did it in a very 2020-way: over Zoom.

These young authors, ages 18–24, started by creating individual characters inspired by their own lived experiences, and then identified the season in which that character would learn and grow. Would their stories take place at the beginning of the shutdown, when no one knew what to expect? Would they be set during the summer, in the wake of George Floyd, when we marched historic streets in support of Black lives? Would their stories take place during the fall, when the election turned the air electric with anticipation? Would they take place during that first hard COVID winter, when isolation was at its worst, and our nation's Capitol faced attack? Or would they live somewhere in between, during those strange, unmoored, and liminal times? We had all lived through so much. What better way to process it all than to do it through story and in community.

At Shout Mouse, our young people always write their books collaboratively. However, with this project, being in community was central to the creative process, as 2020 was a lonely year. We had monthly all-group meetings, where all authors gathered virtually and safely reflected on their own experiences, developed a shared timeline of what took place that year, and looked at and discussed other art responding to 2020. We wanted to ensure that their stories were as emotionally honest as they were historically accurate, a goal that demanded that they not only recall their own experiences, but that they also listened to those of others, fact-checked, and did their research on what took place during that time.

These large group check-ins would become anchors between weekly one-on-one writing sessions, when each author was paired with a professional story coach and where they were able to apply what we discussed to their characters' individual narratives. Then, finally, after ten months of these intensive weekly writing sessions, large group meetings, and thorough editorial sessions thereafter, we had arrived at our goal: a manuscript, titled *What It*

Cost Us: Stories of Pandemic and Protest in DC.

As 2020 unfolded, our city became an epicenter of sorts, not necessarily for viral transmission, but for impact, for cost. What happens when the city — defined by movement, progress, and transience — remains still, stuck even? And, more importantly, what happens to the city's youth? Young people as a population were uniquely affected in 2020. Many of our authors' school years, jobs, college plans, proms, graduations, and general sense of safety were canceled, threatened, or just modified without the magic. These formative years and rites of passage that should have marked their emergence into the world folded under universal crisis, young people's voices muffled beneath the weight.

Still, our authors wrote and spoke up. As they used their voices to create these stories, they also processed their own losses — how, though a disease may not discriminate, a pandemic, an election, and police brutality *certainly* can, each highlighting or augmenting already-existing inequities in health care, employment, political enfranchisement, or just how we connect to one another.

Dear reader, you will see how, though each story is set during various crises of 2020, the stories themselves are about love, trust, understanding, joy, and community — a collective call for a more equitable world and a celebration of what young people like Bilal, Camal, T'Asia, Deyssy, Saylenis, Joseph, Tatiana, Iman, Najae, and Darne'Sha have created in the meantime.

WHAT IT COST US

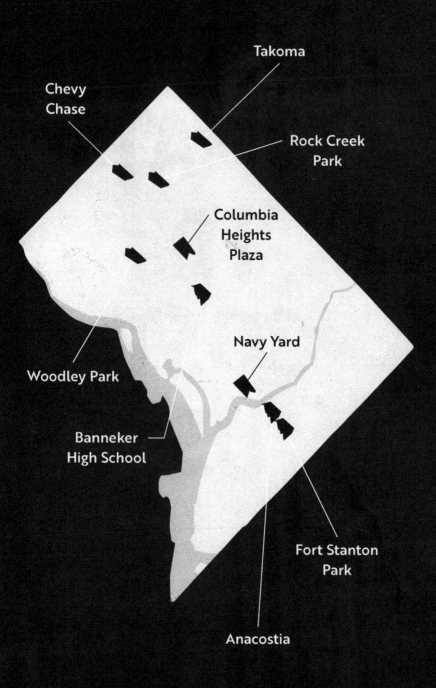

Sunday, March 1, 2020 —●

SPRING

Sunday, May 24, 2020 —●

THE STORM, THE RAINBOW, AND VALENTINA

by Deyssy Mosso

Two Weeks In
Friday, March 27, 2020

It's been two weeks since the world shut down. Two weeks since everything that had been going so right for me started going so very, very wrong.

I am sitting in front of the window of my room, knitting masks with old cloth. I can't find masks at the stores and neither can my mom nor my Tía Gabriela. I am listening to my favorite song, "Hasta la Raíz," by Natalia Lafourcade: "Yo te llevo dentro, hasta la raíz."

Y por más que crezca, vas a estar aquí
Aunque yo me oculte tras la montaña
Y encuentre un campo lleno de caña
No habrá manera, ni rayo de luna
Que tú te vayas

This song has become my companion these past few days; it reminds me of my abuela. When I turn it up loud and I close my eyes, I see her smile, feel her lips touch my forehead. Abuela. My rock, who God took too soon. My only consolation is that she does not have to face the new sickness now raging out there, on the other side of this window.

With these words, I am Valentina. I am from a pueblito in Guerrero, Mexico. I came to America seven years ago, pursuing my American Dream. So far, so… not what I expected. Since I came to America I have been living in Washington, DC: first in an apartment downtown, then in a studio on R Street, where we all crammed together for more than five years. Now, finally, this year, at the age of 20, I moved to live alone. I had to — the apartment that my family and I were renting before only allowed three people to live there. But also, I was ready to start an independent life. How could I have known the isolation that lay ahead?

I now live one block away from the Columbia Heights Plaza. Before the shutdown, from my window I could see and hear the bustle and energy of the events that took place there: the farmers' markets, the voting rights marches, the salsa rueda circles, and children splashing in the fountain. But, I haven't seen or heard any of that now for weeks. Now, I can only see people walking with fear of not being too close to someone else.

My God, what am I going to do?

I really miss my family, Tía Gabriela, my friends, and the people in the community who I always helped and who helped me. In a few days, I have to pay for many things — my rent, more groceries, tuition — and I almost have no money left. Honestly, I feel sad, but I have to be strong and not give up. I am Valentina, the girl who never gives up. I come from a strong family who does not give up. If we did, how would we be here?

Back in the Day

My abuela taught us not to give up. She was born in the
same pueblito as me. Her parents had nine babies and she
was the only baby girl my bisabuelos had. We lived with
her in Mexico and she always shared her stories with us.
I still remember one of her stories, that when she was still
very small, her mother taught her how to make tortillas
and do laundry. Her mother would tell her, "Ya estás
grande para que me ayudes con las labores de la casa." And
so, even as a little girl, she helped with the house chores.

My abuela didn't go to school. She learned how to
count, and one of her brothers taught her how to read a
little bit, but her parents said girls should be at home. A
woman's responsibility was to take care of the house and
the kids, while the men went out to work. I loved my
abuela, but I'm glad I wasn't raised like her, and I'm glad
she didn't raise my mom or Tía Gabriela like her either.
My abuelita taught them how to be strong and brave. They
are not the type to give up easily.

Mami and Tía Gabriela come from eight babies that
my abuela had. Tía Gabriela was the sixth, and she was
kind and friendly. Mami was the youngest and surprisingly
very serious. They were the only sisters next to six brothers.
My abuela did teach them how to cook and do laundry, but
she also taught them how to work hard on the farm. They
learned how to grow all kinds of vegetables that they would
later sell or keep for the family. The days were long and hot

with their hands covered in dirt and blisters. My abuelo seemed to never like this, shaking his head whenever he saw my mami or Tía Gabriela carrying an armful of vegetables. But he never complained when the soups came out just right, thanks to the fresh food they grew.

Still, Tía Gabriela and Mami didn't want to work in the fields forever. They really wanted to go to school, but that was something my abuelo really would not allow. The first and only time my abuela asked him to let the girls go to school, he stormed out of the house and slept at his brother's house for the night. So my abuela never asked him again, and Mami and Tía Gabriela never went to school. Instead, my abuela would have her youngest son, Diego, read to the girls at night and teach them whatever he learned that day. Eventually, Mami and Tía Gabriela learned how to read. They could also do math, and they knew about the history of Mexico. I don't think my abuelo ever found out.

It wasn't until she was 28 years old that Tía Gabriela left for the United States. Money was tight and there were no jobs in their pueblito, while the cities were too dangerous for a single woman. She left by herself, joining a group of strangers who each had their own reasons for leaving. Four years later, my parents decided Mexico was no longer a place where we could live. The education was not what my parents wanted for us, the jobs didn't pay enough to properly feed a family, and there was simply no future for us there. It was the hardest decision ever, and also our only choice. So my parents, siblings, and I all packed what we could into some backpacks, and we left for the United States to join my Tía Gabriela.

I was 13 years old when I came to the United States. We didn't have much money, but our neighbors had given us lots of food to help us along the way. Doña Carolina packed us sandwiches and cookies, while Don Fernando from down the street gave us a bag of fruit. Many of the neighbors said they would pray for us and they gave us the names of their relatives in case we needed a place to stay along the way. It took us two weeks to cross the border from my pueblito to Texas. I was scared, especially right before we reached the border. I had heard so many stories of people getting lost or people going to jail and I didn't want that for me or anyone in my family, but, at the same, I had to do it. I wanted to go to school to help my family and to help other people, just like they helped us.

I'll never forget how nice those people were to us. It showed me how much a small gesture can mean to someone. I mean when you think about a piece of fruit now, it may seem like nothing, but, when you've been walking in the hot sun for five days straight, a bite of fruit is a bite of heaven. Since then, I promised myself I would give back however I could.

Family Dinner
Sunday, March 1, 2020

Not long before the shutdown, I had my first night
training as a host at my new job, Él Bebe. It was a
restaurant down in Navy Yard. I remember being so
happy because it had almost been a month that I was
without a job. I had to quit my last one because the
manager was giving me too many duties and he didn't
want to pay me more. But my new manager for this job
was so different. His starting pay was already more than
what I was making before, and that didn't include tips
or overtime. I was so happy. I called my mom almost
immediately after my training.

"Hello Mami, how are you?" I could feel myself smiling
as I spoke. "I have very good news: I have a new job as a
host! Now, I'll be able to pay my tuition and my rent!" I
said, trying to speak over my mom's excited screams.

"Congratulations, hija, for your new job," she said as
her throat lumped up and her voice began to break. "I told
you they would give you the job. You are a very hard-
working and strong woman. Your brothers and your Tía
Gabriela are in the house and we have cooked your favorite
food, golden tacos."

As soon as I heard my mom say tacos, my mouth
started to water. "Gracias, Mami. I can be there in forty
minutes. Right now I'm waiting for the Metro at the Navy
Yard para ir a su casa."

Thirty-eight minutes later to be exact, I was walking through my mom's front door and I could smell the hot beef in the air. I couldn't wait to swallow all the tacos that could fit in my stomach. Within minutes, the three tacos Mami had served me were gone.

"Ma, what delicious tacos you cooked," I said. Mi mami is a woman who loves to cook and it shows. She smiled and wiped her hands across her apron.

"I really like my new job so far, Mami. The manager told me that they will give me five days a week to work, and once I get my first check, I'll be able to pay half of my rent and my books."

Ma said, "Qué bueno, mijita, gracias a Dios que ya tienes trabajo. It is a true blessing to have a job. I am so happy for you."

We finished the dinner and Mami brought us some chocolate caliente. Hot chocolate was one of my favorites.

Once everyone had their cup of hot chocolate, Ma asked, "Vale, can you turn on the TV? Let's watch some novelas."

I turned on the TV, but instead of watching novelas, I left it on the news.

"COVID-19 cases continue to overwhelm hospitals in Italy, the new epicenter of the disease."

Tía Gabriela shook her head in doubt, saying, "I don't think the virus will be such a problem here. At least I hope not."

Earlier that day, I had heard two ladies saying the

same thing on the Metro.

"Sí, no creo que sea tan grave. Estamos bien," Mami said, assuring us we would be okay.

I hoped they were right, because I had a lot of exciting things in the weeks ahead. "Hey, did you remember that the annual youth summit is coming up?" I said.

"Oh, yes, how nice!" said Tía Gabriela. "You're helping to plan that, right?"

"Well, sort of. I'm speaking on one of the panels, but I wouldn't say I'm planning the whole thing. LAYC and Montgomery County are doing most of that."

"What is that exactly?" asked Mami.

"It's basically a day to help immigrant youth integrate into the schools here, like connecting them with after-school programs, telling them about ESL classes, and helping them apply for scholarships. I think this is only their second year doing it."

"Vale, can we go with you to the youth summit?" my little siblings yelled all at once.

"Claro que sí pueden ir conmigo. I don't see why not. Actually, would you guys like to help me practice? I have a little less than a week to prepare my speech."

The kids all yelled in excitement and I couldn't stop laughing.

This is the moment I keep going back to in my mind, when I had so much to look forward to. How could we have known that all our enthusiasm — and assumptions of safety — would so soon be snatched away?

Headlines

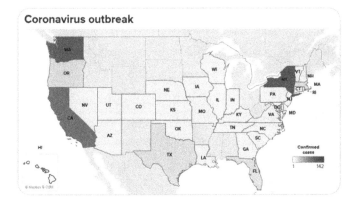

Coronavirus outbreak

CDC reports 142 confirmed cases of COVID-19 across the U.S.

March 3, 2020

District of Columbia announces its first COVID-19 case, a Reverend at Christ Church Georgetown

March 7, 2020

Emergency
Wednesday, March 11, 2020

The mayor declared a public health emergency in DC. I'm not sure what that means, but it doesn't sound good. There are talks of shutting down events, closing businesses, and people working from home. Immediately, I think about my job. The manager told everyone the restaurant would be closed today. He said maybe in a few days I could continue my training. But, in my mind, the only thing I can think is, *What will happen if they close everything for more than just a few days?* I can't afford to live without a job.

I try going on Facebook to distract myself, but post after post is talking about the coronavirus. Every post or news article talks about the shutting down of restaurants and canceling of events. I just saw one post from LAYC saying, "Due to the declared public health emergency in DC, we, unfortunately, are postponing our annual youth summit. We are still working on a new date. Once we have that clarified, we will let you know." Great, I have been practicing my speech for weeks and now who knows if it will happen. It's just not fair.

My heart is beating faster. I take a deep breath.

I swipe out of the app and click on Instagram, hoping to see something different, and it's even worse. More and more bad news. My cousin in Florida just posted saying the restaurant where she works has closed due to the public emergency. A lot of people are commenting, saying, "The governor in my state announced a public health emergency, too… A lot of people are already closing their businesses… Time to stock up on food… This is a serious problem."

While I'm scrolling on my phone, I get a text from my Tía Gabriela. "Mija, ¿cómo estás? Do you have enough food? Your mother said the stores near you might still have something for you to pick up. Let me know if you need anything."

Instagram is not making me feel better, so I should just get out of my social media and go to the store to buy things to eat. I should also look for masks and things like hand sanitizer, although I doubt I'll find that.

I go on my way to Panam Supermarket. It's not too far from my home — just four blocks away — and it's definitely worth the walk. I always find everything I need there, and it all comes from Latin America.

As I'm walking, I notice the streets are too quiet and there are not many people walking. *Is it because of what the mayor announced, or because of the fear of the virus that people are protecting themselves in their homes?* Either way, I have no option to stay home, so I continue on my way.

When I get closer to the store I see a police car outside Panam. I wonder what could be happening. My body begins to sweat, and even my hands feel wet. My heart is still pounding. I take two deep breaths this time, trying to calm down.

I now see many people rushing out of Panam with their shopping carts very full. The only people not moving are a couple sitting on the curb in handcuffs. One officer is on the phone, while another officer is holding a bottle of hand sanitizer and disinfectant wipes. *What is happening?* Once I get inside, Panam is overflowing with people. There are so many people, Dios mio, aquí no se puede caminar. I can't even take one step without bumping into someone, or getting pushed.

In the distance, I hear some ladies yelling, "That toilet paper packet is mine! I grabbed it first!" A man behind me says, "Son, go outside and grab four gallons of water." The manager to my far left is talking to an older woman: "Señora, entienda, we don't have any more masks. The last masks were sold yesterday. Please calm down."

Now I understand why the police car is outside. I also understand I need to hurry up if I want to buy anything worth getting.

I have only fifty dollars, but I'm able to buy some canned food and two gallons of water. I don't find any masks or toilet paper, but I decide not to venture into any other stores — it's too overwhelming. I just text Tía Gabriela back, letting her know I'm okay. At this point, I just want to go home.

I finally arrive at my quiet apartment and take the bags to my bedroom. Under my bed, I have three boxes where I put canned food. *Vale, you still have beans, canned fruit, pasta, and canned tomato sauce. I hope I bought enough food for the days ahead…*

2:02

District of Columbia Shutdown, Trump Declares Nationwide Emergency

March 13, 2020

DC Government Closes Bars + Restaurants, Begins Takeout/ Delivery Service Only

March 16, 2020

DC's First COVID-19 Death is Announced

March 20, 2020

Swipe to unlock

Locked In
Monday, March 23, 2020

It's 5:50 a.m., and I'm wide awake. The only thing I hear are cars and ambulances passing by. I can't sleep — my eyes are too irritated, and I have a headache. It's dark still, but soon the sun will rise, with its rays of bright light. I can already start to see a faint glow at my window, but I can't move. My body is glued to the bed.

It's been over a week since DC officially shut down, and I haven't left my apartment. I have never been so anxious. Honestly, I have been thinking too much about how I'm going to pay my rent and the rest of my tuition. *Online classes start today. Should I join? I don't even know if my laptop is charged. I've only used Zoom once before.* The restaurant still hasn't opened back up, so I don't have a job. *Maybe I can go live with Mami again. No, there's no way I can do that.*

Everything Mayor Bowser has said since she announced the shutdown hasn't helped me, and I don't know what to do. The youth summit was officially canceled, not just postponed. No one knows when (or if?) this will end.

I think about taking some big breaths since that has helped me to not give up in the past, but even that sounds like too much right now. Instead I think about my almost-empty refrigerator and my almost-empty wallet. *The food in my boxes won't last me forever. How long are we going to be like this?*

More than anything, I hope my family is okay. Please God don't leave me alone. Don't leave my family alone. *We did not make this long journey just to be trapped, alone, a few miles apart. I feel terrible and I don't know how long I will be here without seeing my familia, my friends, Tía Gabriela, everyone. It's just too much for me.*

A bit of sunshine starts to peek through the window just as my eyes get too heavy for me to keep open.

It's now 2:00 p.m. and I am still in bed. My room is now bright and filled with sunlight. I should have invested in some curtains. It looks like my mom and Tía Gabriela have called and texted multiple times: "Mija, ¿cómo estás? Do you need anything? We have some eggs and arepas. Do you want us to drop some off to you?"

I just close my phone and drop it back on the floor. I don't feel like answering and I'm not hungry anyways. If I don't even have energy to stand up, how could I have the energy to eat? All I can think over and over again is, *What am I going to do?* A few weeks ago, I had a good job, I was going to be a speaker in the youth summit, and I was enjoying my first apartment by myself. Now, I don't have a job, the youth summit is canceled, and I'm not sure if I'll even be able to pay this month's rent.

Tía Gabriela calls again. I don't pick up and instead

think about our last conversation. A few days ago, when I told her the youth summit was canceled, all she told me was, "You have the ability to change many things if you put your mind to it. You are very brave, Valentina. Remember that."

Right now, those words sound empty to me. Instead, I just turn over, close my eyes, and go back to sleep.

I wake up and the first thing I see is darkness. I can only see the streetlight outside, casting shadows in my room. I see I left my window open, so that explains why my room is so cold. My body is stiff and I realize I spent the whole day in bed. *Well, Vale, let's try to move a little bit.* I decide the roof might be a good idea, so I grab some blankets, two bananas, and a bottle of water to head out the door.

I almost walk over a big, brown paper bag. I open it to find arepas, eggs, bread, meat, and some fruits. I immediately know this is from my Tía Gabriela, and my eyes begin to water, but I don't let myself cry. I shake my head, bring the bag inside, and continue to the roof. It's not too cold tonight, just a very light wind that comes and goes. The sky looks so bright and the moon looks gigantic. For a moment, I wonder if I could almost touch it. I remember, as my abuela told me, "La luna siempre estará contigo vayas a donde vayas." I then think about the last family dinner we had at Mami's house. Those tacos were so good, and Tía Gabriela was there. That night was like this with a bright, big moon.

I take a deep breath, and feel the expanse of the world around me. So many people are struggling under these same stars. I remind myself: *I am not the only one who is going through these things.* I know I'm really not alone.

Thank you, Tía Gabriela
Tuesday, March 24, 2020

It's the following morning and I'm making an omelet with some of the eggs my tía brought me. The phone rings and it's her. That's when I remember I never called her back yesterday. She must be worried.

"Hello, Tía Gabriela," I say.

"Hi mija, how are you?" says Tía Gabriela. Her voice is sweet and it bounces just like her chocolate-colored curls. She's waiting for me to speak, but I don't know what to answer.

"I'm okay," I finally say. "I got the package you left for me. Me estoy preparando unos huevos." My voice trails off.

There is a pause before Tía Gabriela speaks again. If she were standing in front of me, I would feel her eyes piercing me until I tell her what is really going on, but I keep quiet. It's almost as if I am avoiding eye contact… just through the phone.

"Mija, do you need something?" This time her voice is softer and less upbeat, but more smooth like a velvet river.

"Tía Gabriela," I almost whisper. "To be honest, it's been hard not seeing my family, my friends, and you. Yesterday, I woke up just wishing everything would go back to the way it was before."

"I know, mija. I also want to go back," Tía Gabriela says. "But, unfortunately, we can't. We need to be strong and brave to keep praying for us to be okay. You are not alone, mija. I am here to help you, but remember you need to stay positive and not give up either. Why don't you find something to do with this free time you have? You like to read and make crafts. You can try new things."

We talk for a little while longer until my tía says my eggs are going to get cold. When we hang up, I only eat a bite of my omelet before I look to my sewing materials, the fabric I have pulled together for making masks. It feels so small in the face of so much fear, but it is something.

In that moment, I begin to get to work. I take small bites of my omelet as I cut fabric and sew pieces together. With each stitch, I don't feel so hopeless.

The Rainbow
Friday, March 27, 2020. Again.

Which brings me back to this moment, two weeks in:

I'm sitting in the front window of my room, listening to "Hasta La Raíz," knitting masks. It's morning. At this time on a normal day, kids would be on their way to school. People would be on their way to work. Vendedores would be setting up their stands to sell their products on the street. But today, like most days these days, everything is quiet. I only see a señora walking with her two children.

She's talking on the phone and I hear her saying how she didn't find any masks at the stores. She looks worried and desperate, while her children's faces look sad. The little girl is crying and her mother tells her not to touch her face or she can get COVID. Now, I think I understand what Tía Gabriela meant. Her words flash in my mind:

"You have the ability to change many things if you put your mind to it. You are very brave, Valentina."

She was right. I know what I need to do.

I yell out of my window. "¡Oiga, Señora! ¡Señora, espere! Wait! I have some masks I can give you."

I quickly run to the box in my closet and grab four masks. For the past few days I have been spending my time making masks, and now I have a pile of them, ready to share. It felt good to make these, reminding me of my promise to myself as a young girl, to give back however I could.

I put the masks in a Ziploc bag and run down the stairs. When I get outside, I motion to the woman and put down the bag for her to grab. I keep my distance, leaving it by the entrance to our building's front yard. I call out to her, "These masks are for you."

She doesn't move and just looks at me with tears in her eyes. Her kids look up at her confused. I give her a moment, but she is still in shock.

"Take them. Venga," I say.

Finally, she moves to grab the Ziploc bag. "Muchas gracias, muchacha," she says, her voice breaking. She takes out one mask for each of them and puts the extra mask away in her own bag.

Seeing this woman's gratitude for the masks fills me with joy and hope. I realize I can do more with my time than be sad in bed all day. Abuela used to say, "No importa tan fuerte sea la tormenta, al final siempre saldrá un arcoiris." I don't know how long this storm will last, and I'm not sure when the rainbow will show, but I know I can actually help people. And I am reminded that small gestures can mean so much.

I go back to my box of old cloth, grab some bright ones, and sit at my sewing machine. It's time to get to work.

NOT WHAT I SIGNED UP FOR

by T'Asia Bates

The Problems Begin
Saturday, April 18, 2020

My closet fits into six huge black trash bags. One bag
for summer clothes, one for spring, one for fall, one for
winter… and, of course two bags full of shoes.

Eyebrows raised, side-eye, shaking his head, Dad gives
me "the look" as he carries my stuff to the car. I know I
should help, but he would just complain about how slow
I move anyway. Dad stuffs three bags in the backseat and
three bags in the trunk before getting into the driver's
seat. From the passenger's seat, I look up at my house only
to see my two younger brothers waving at me from the
window. My mom, not there. Probably in her room… still
ignoring me.

Breathing heavily, Dad wipes sweat from his forehead and says nothing. Even though I'm only moving a couple miles away, it's going to be a long drive… It's going to be a long year.

Since Dad won't say anything, let me introduce myself: my name is Xzavia, pronounced Zah-Vee-Uh (yes, the 'X' is silent). Last name: Amor, which means love, but I haven't been lucky in that department these days…

It is April of 2020, two months before I am scheduled to graduate from Banneker High School. I should be attending school in-person, I should know where I'm going to college next year, I should be preparing senior year events with my best friends Richard and Rock, and coordinating prom outfits with my boyfriend Quincy. I should still be living with my mom, my 1-year-old baby brother Harlin, and my 12-year-old brother Kayden, in our cream-colored house on Georgia Ave NW.

Instead, I'm struggling through virtual high school, I haven't decided what I'm going to do next year, I haven't seen my best friends in over a month, and Quincy and I are having problems. Instead, my grades are falling, and mom is making me move in with my dad, step-mom, and 11-year-old step sister.

See? Not much here to love…

When we pull up to the old brick apartment building in Anacostia, my dad turns off the car and turns to me. "Just be chill," he says. He is a man of few words, but I know he means "don't start nothin' with your step-mom and step-sister." I look at him and roll my eyes. *As long as they're 'chill' with me,* I think.

My step-mom is named Ashley. She's a 35-year-old stay-at-home mom and lives in her Adidas athleisure. She always wears a long, low ponytail and a smug, bougie expression that stains her caramel complexion. She's waiting in the living room with a big tray of sugar cookies. She knows they're my favorite. *Um… What is she trying to do?* I think, but I manage to drag out a "Thanks."

I decide to reach for a cookie, but Ashley looks at my hands with disgust and tilts her head toward the sink. "You want me to wash my hands?" I ask.

"That would be nice," Ashley responds.

"It's not like I have *it*," I say, annoyed, as I walk slowly to the kitchen sink and wash my hands, looking at her until she seems pleased.

My step-sister Reagan is too busy playing Fortnite on her PlayStation to notice that I've walked in. Ashley nudges her. "Oh, hey," she says dryly before returning to her game. She has dreadlocks that fall to the middle of her back, the same caramel complexion as her mom, and wears cool, hipster glasses. She's got style, but I wouldn't dare tell her that. "Hey," I say back before walking past the tray of cookies and heading to my new room.

As soon as I close the door, I let out a heavy sigh. I feel like I've been holding my breath ever since Dad picked me up. I take a look at the bland, beige walls, and realize not even the room seems to fit me.

I push my bags into the corner and sit on my bed. I want to forget everything I went through. I take out my sketchbook and pencils, and start to draw.

I start on the Boyfriend jeans. Lapis Blue. Distress at the knees. Then the top. Something black. Hooded. Dark. Tight sleeves, a skull and crossbones on the back. I title it "The Day of the Dead" before hiding the book under my mattress, where no one would ever look.

Damn! I promised my friends I would text them when I settled in. I open up the group chat:

The P.I.T.

Xzavia

GUYS!

Richard

Yo

Rock

So… how was it?

Xzavia

Stressful.

Rock

Just take it one day at a time.

You know you got us too.

Richard

Facts

Ever since I met Richard and Rock in 9th grade, they have always been there for me. Even when everyone else — fake friends, teachers, family — lets us down, we always show up. That's why we call our group chat "The P.I.T." — *People I Tolerate.*

Even though I haven't seen them in over a month, we make sure to talk every day. I place my phone on the dresser, feeling reassured that I have people in my corner.

Mom 101
Monday, April 20, 2020

KNOCK! KNOCK! I am startled awake.

"Wake up, Xzavia! It's already 7:30!" Ashley says enthusiastically.

"School doesn't even start until 8:45!" I scream.

"You missed dinner last night, and you need to eat! Remember, breakfast is the most important meal of the day," Ashley responds, dismissing my grumpiness.

I brush my teeth, wash my face, and move sluggishly to the dining room. Reagan is already seated and dressed. "Hi," she says, almost sarcastically. I say nothing; I am too amazed by the full table: waffles, eggs, turkey bacon, strawberries, pineapple, and OJ. Breakfast at my mom's house was just cereal-and-go. "Wow, thank you," I say to Ashley who is in the kitchen, getting a head start on cleaning.

I sit down and start piling food on my empty plate. My stomach growls loudly. I feel like I haven't eaten in forever. I didn't mean to miss dinner last night, but I was exhausted from the long day. Not to mention, dinner would've probably been awkward anyway... This breakfast certainly is.

Reagan and I sit across from each other, avoiding eye contact. All we hear is the constant clinking of forks on our plates. Even if I felt like talking, I wouldn't know what to say:

Why is your mom so annoying?

Why did you steal my dad?

Will you ever feel like my sister?

I look at the clock above the dining room table. 8:40 a.m. *OMG!* I quickly finish eating, clean up my mess, and go to my room to get my computer set up. One of the only good things about being here is that I have my own space to focus on virtual school.

At the start of the pandemic, virtual school was hectic. I was still at my mom's and had to take care of my younger brother Kayden, making sure that he ate and went to his classes. Mom always used me as a free babysitter. I'm still a teenager. How could I take care of other people when I was still trying to take care of myself?

Meanwhile, my other brother, Harlin, was one year old, and he would cry so loud you could hear him all the way down the street. But he wasn't down the street, he was in the room right next to mine. Some nights, he'd cry incessantly, disturbing my sleep. It wasn't long until I started missing classes, and my grades started slipping.

One day, my teacher, Mr. Hernandez, called my mom:

"Ms. Amor, I'm calling to inform you that Xzavia hasn't been attending class, and I'm worried. I know this is a difficult time for everyone, but it has been a week since I've last seen her. We have to make a plan for her to show up so that it doesn't affect her graduation."

After that, my mom told me to pack, that I was moving in with my dad. I wanted to say, *But this is your fault! I was trying to help you!* I stayed silent instead, and started getting my stuff together. I haven't spoken to her since.

It Keeps Goin': Heartbreak
Tuesday, April 28, 2020 — a week later

"¡Buenos Dias! ¿Cómo estás?" Mr. Hernandez says excitedly. I snap back to the present.

Why are adults so enthusiastic and extra in the morning? Like... chill out.

Mr. Hernandez starts his lesson on conjugation.

"Today we are going to talk about the conditional tense..."

Before, when I was living with mom, I'd be annoyed by a new subject. But today, I feel surprisingly determined. And, also surprisingly, the whole class is smooth sailing. I'm able to focus the entire time. I have no obnoxiously loud children to worry about and no hectic commotion going on in the background. I also stay for the entire class, which I've never done before! I mean like... NEVER. The work seems easier than before, too... but is it the work, or is it the fact that I no longer have any distractions?

Also a first: I manage to finish school that day with no attitude. I feel at peace.

Until...

Quincy <3

Quincy<3:

Hey babe.

My boyfriend's name pops up on my phone. We've been together for almost a year, and until recently, we talked every day. I thought about him every second. But as the shutdown started and continued, and now *continues*, we haven't been able to see each other AT ALL. In fact, we've barely even spoken since I've moved, making me feel even more alone than when I got here. When we thought this was only going to be two weeks, we thought we could get through. But between getting my grades back up for senior year and this "Big Bad," everything has gotten so hard.

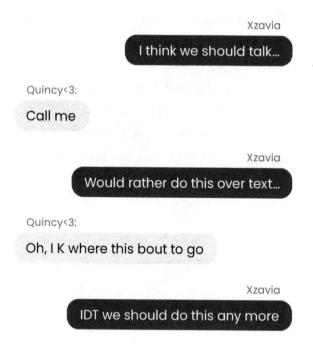

Xzavia

I think we should talk...

Quincy<3:

Call me

Xzavia

Would rather do this over text...

Quincy<3:

Oh, I K where this bout to go

Xzavia

IDT we should do this any more

Quincy<3:

We could try to work things out

It's just a lots goin on rn

Xzavia

I feel like we've tried already

It's still not working

Quincy<3 is typing…

Quincy<3 is typing…

Quincy<3:

I understand

I feel bad about lying to him about not being able to talk, but it would be too painful to hear his voice. I loved Quincy a lot, and still do, so the fact that we should end our relationship hurts.

I pull out my sketchbook from under the mattress and start to draw: This time, a gray sweatsuit. The pants are loose-fitted, almost like they belong to someone else. A paste-colored velvet stripe along the sides just to keep the glam in the glum.

Now, the top: Same gray. Cropped at the belly, long sleeves that go past the fingers. The words "Heartbreak" written in block letters using the same white velvet.

I look the new design over and title it: "The End."

People I Tolerate...
Saturday, May 2, 2020 — 2 weeks after moving in

The next few days I feel lost. Time drags and stretches. Every second feels like a millennium.

I try to distract myself with school. And even though my grades are improving, I have to pretend not to feel like a wilting rose, like I'm not eating endless ice cream. But whenever anyone tries to talk to me, they sound like they're underwater.

Part of me wishes my mom were here. This is something I should be able to go to my mom about, but instead...

"Sweetheart," Ashley pokes her head through the door, "you've barely come out of your room. What's going on?"

One of her eyebrows is raised. Her eyes look genuine, concerned.

I turn my head away from her and towards the wall.

"You have more life to live, Xzavia. Don't dwell on this moment. If you want to talk, you know where to find me."

She doesn't mean that. She's just trying to be nice, I think, before I let the depression put me back to sleep.

When I wake up, it's Saturday and I feel good enough to get out of bed. *I need some fresh air,* I think, and put on my favorite hoodie and jogger set. When I walk outside, I finally feel like I can breathe. The air is cool and crisp, a perfect DC morning. I walk to Fort Stanton Park around the corner and open up the group chat.

The P.I.T.

Rock

Where have u been?

Richard

Kill

Rock

Hellllllllllllllo??

Richard

Kill

Rock

Zavi, u ok?

My screen is full of Rock being extra and Richard using his lowkey DC slang. Typical.

Xzavia

My fault. Been goin thru it. Me n Quincy broke up

Richard

Dang

Rock

Whaaaaaaattttttt??!!!🫣

Xzavia

It's been rly hard, u guys.
I miss u guys

Richard

Damn girl, that's crazy but imy2

Rock

We miss u too. We was rly worried
abt u and I'm sorry abt u and old
dude. We'll ttyl remember u will
always be okay Zavi.

I sigh with relief, put in my AirPods, turn on Summer Walker's "Over It," and slide my phone back into my hoodie pocket. After the words of encouragement from my friends, I feel better enough to walk back home. Maybe things will be alright after all. Except...

...And the People I DON'T
Still Saturday, May 2, 2020

When I walk into the house, I run into Reagan, who's quickly trying to walk out. Something tells me to take a swift glance at her outfit because you know I can't have anybody associated with me looking a mess. But when I look at her I can tell she's nervous. She has a blank expression on her face, and beads of sweat drip down her forehead like raindrops. And then I see it.

Reagan has on my white, oversized, $390, Amiri x Playboy collab shirt. My eyes immediately see red. I'm livid.

"Why the hell do you have my shirt on, Reagan!?"

Sometimes I don't realize when I'm missing clothes because I have so many. So, these past few weeks when I couldn't find specific pieces of clothing — it's happened a few times now — I just assumed they were buried somewhere with the rest of my wardrobe. Now, I realize that Reagan has been digging through my closet and stealing my stuff! And not just any of my stuff, but the *expensive* stuff.

"C'mon, Xzavia, please let me wear this," she pleads. "It's not like you were really going to wear it soon. You have all those clothes."

"Reagan, you better be fucking joking! Like seriously I know my eyes are deceiving me right now. Why are you wearing my stuff? I should literally smack you right now! Do you know how much that shirt cost, girl?"

"GIRLS! WHAT ARE YOU DOING?" Ashley
screams as she charges out of *my* room.

"Oh nah! What are YOU doing in MY room?" I ask,
turning my head and walking towards her.

"This is still MY house, young lady. I can be wherever
I want in MY house. And, maybe if you cleaned your
room once in a while, I wouldn't have to make your bed
and pick up after you."

I start to worry when I hear her say "bed." I run
straight for my room. I don't even tell Reagan to take the
shirt off or anything.

I see my fashion sketchbook open to the page with the
prom dress on it on my newly-made bed. I designed this
dress back in August, at the beginning of the school year.
Caramel mesh, fitted everywhere, a long train, rhinestones
along the bosom. I titled it "A Night to Remember." Back
then, before the shutdown, when I designed this dress, I
thought of course there'd be a prom. I thought I'd be going
with Quincy. I thought it'd be the time when everyone
would turn their heads to look at *me*. Now, when I look at
it, I wanna title it "SIKE!"

The worst things keep happening to me...

"Why are you going through my stuff, bro?" I say with
a scarily calm anger, holding up the designs that I didn't
want anyone to see.

"I didn't know you were even into fashion!" Ashley
says energetically. "Maybe if you spent more energy on
these drawings and less on cursing at your sister, you'd be

a happier person."

"YOU'VE NEVER CARED ABOUT WHAT
I'M INTO. Y'ALL NEVER PAY ATTENTION TO
ME ANYWAY. ALL YOU DO IS NAG AND BE
FAKE, ALL REAGAN DOES IS PLAY HER GAMES,
AND MY DAD WORKS SO MUCH IT'S AS IF HE
DOESN'T EXIST."

My voice cracks like a scratched record. My eyes feel
heavy, as if they're waiting for someone to turn a knob, a
faucet waiting for a little more pressure to turn water from
a pool to a rapid. Before I know it, I'm tasting salt. Tears
are running down my cheeks.

I haven't cried since I was 10, when Dad moved out. I
tasted the same salt when I watched him slam our front door.

And just as I think that, my dad walks in through the
door looking confused and stuck. He's wearing his work
uniform. It looks like a custom Dickie outfit. It's been like
a week since I've actually seen him. I'm usually asleep by
the time he comes home.

"What's going on here, girls?" he says. Clearly he's
trying to understand why I'm crying. And of course here
comes Ashley, jumping on the opportunity to tell him
everything that's been going on.

Ashley whines something to my dad about my
"profanity" and my "sassy, over-the-top attitude."

"Now Xzavia, why are you cursing at Reagan and yelling
at Ashley? I work hard every day to keep things functioning
around here, and you wanna start unnecessary commotion!"

Here we go again. Like dude, you have to be kidding me.

I try to get two words out and all he does is continue to yell.

"DIDN'T I TELL YOU WHEN YOU CAME HERE THAT YOU NEEDED TO CHILL?"

"Right, so am I really the one who needs to chill here? Reagan felt like it was okay to go through my stuff and take something very expensive and PLEASE don't let me get started on your wife. SHE felt like it was okay to go through my personal belongings, things I don't like sharing with anyone."

My crying is hysterical at this point. I start to lose it.

"You don't know WHAT goes on in this house, Dad," I say. "You're literally NEVER here."

My dad keeps trying to stick up for Ashley, and for his new daughter.

"YOU'RE LITERALLY NEVER HERE!" I repeat.

My father's anger slowly leaves his face, revealing a softer version of him. I watch him try to think of what to say, but fail.

Silence.

Reagan slowly takes off my shirt. Now only a white tank top covers her scrawny body. She hands it back to me. I look at Ashley's washed-out, shocked face. I turn around, go to my room, and close the door. I feel weak. Why can't I ever catch a break?

Safe Haven
Still Saturday, May 2, 2020

I don't understand why things keep happening to me. I'm
angry. I don't understand how things keep getting so bad.
I'm trying to be better. I'm trying to adjust. I'm trying to
feel my best, but I am slowly wilting away, getting to a
point where I can't take this unbelievable stress and pain.
And what do I have to look forward to, anyway? It's the
end of my senior year, but there's no prom. No late nights
with friends. No graduation — no real one, anyway.
It's like everything has been stolen from me. And I'm
beginning to think I won't ever get it back.

I need something that feels normal. I take my phone
out of my pocket, and instead of texting "The P.I.T.", I
FaceTime them, needing to see people who feel more like
my family.

Rock answers first with his usual theatrical self.
"Ayyyeeee, Zavi!! Long time no—"

He sees my face, and knows something's wrong.

Richard answers. "Yo, wassup?"

"Zavi, what's wrong?" Rock asks, concerned.

"I just feel so broken, you know? Like nothing is going
to be okay. My whole world is falling apart, and my family
can't even be there for me. I mean, why doesn't my dad ever
choose me? Actually, NO ONE ever chooses me. I haven't
even heard from my mother," I say, feeling the dried tears
crack on my skin as I speak. "Where do I even belong?"

One thing I love about Richard and Rock is they let me speak.

They listen to me unleash, nodding and sympathetic, until I fall asleep.

I Know I'm Not Trippin'!
Sunday, May 3 – Thursday, May 7, 2020

Sunday morning, when I walk to the breakfast table, I see three different boxes of cereal: Frosted Flakes, Honey Nut Cheerios, and Raisin Bran. Which is strange because: 1) There's usually a HUGE breakfast on the table in the morning, and 2) She added Raisin Bran as one of the options. *Why would I ever eat Raisin Bran?! WHO even eats raisins?!*

I pick up the box of Frosted Flakes and pour so much into the bowl that you'd think I was eating for three people. Last night, I spent dinner crying on FaceTime with "The P.I.T.", so I didn't eat. I realize that I'm sitting at the table alone for the first time since I got here. No Reagan sitting across from me all weird and awkward. No Ashley cleaning the kitchen in the efficient yet meticulous way she always does…

Everybody must be avoiding me because of the night before. Tuh! Guess I'm right about nobody caring about me…

I spend the rest of my Sunday doing homework and enjoying my own space.

The next few days continue on, quieter and stranger than normal. On Monday, I notice Reagan staring at me from a distance, looking… I don't know… excited? …pensive? … curious? just dumb? I don't know WHAT you would call that face. All I know is when I stare back, Reagan quickly turns her head, pretending like she wasn't looking at me, picking at what looks like glitter glue stuck to her fingers.

Then, in the middle of the night on Tuesday, I start to hear what sounds like instructional YouTube videos coming from my Dad and Ashley's room. I can't make out what the video is saying, but I assume it's just one of Ashley's many projects. *But why is she working this late?*

My dad starts acting weird too. First of all, he's around more than usual. Second, he keeps trying to make small talk with me like I wasn't just yelling in his face the other day. He asks me about my grades, asks me if I've had a good day, even tries talking to me about the weather. On Wednesday, he actually asks me what I'm doing on Friday, that he'd "like to have a deep conversation about what happened the other day."

Despite my panic, I still push out "Okay."

The last straw is on Thursday, when I see Dad, Ashley, AND Reagan huddled in the kitchen and whispering… *I don't understand WHAT is goin' on, but it's startin' to blow me.* "WHY Y'ALL BEEN ACTIN' WEIRD ALL WEEK?" I finally ask, frustrated.

My dad looks caught off-guard. "Oh, we're just talking about what we're going to eat tonight," he says before they all vanish into their separate spaces like a magic trick.

Weirdos…

The Problems End
Friday, May 8, 2020

KNOCK! KNOCK! It's Friday at 6 o'clock. Dad must be wanting to have his "deep conversation."

"Come in," I say. My hands start to shake. I don't know what he's going to say. *What if he wants to kick me out too?*

Dad pokes his head through the door with a cheesy grin on his face. "Get yourself together and look nice. We're going somewhere."

"Where *exactly*?" I ask. 1) Because we are in the middle of a shutdown, so where we gonna go? and 2) Because no matter what, I have to wear certain outfits for certain places.

"Just come on," he says.

I get in and out of the shower and slick my hair up into a topknot bun. Now for makeup. I put on a little mascara, shape my eyebrows, and put on a nude lipstick with a brown liner — my everyday going-out look.

Now what am I going to wear? I open my closet and my mouth drops. Hanging on the closet door is a familiar fitted caramel mesh with a long train and rhinestones — it's the dress that I created in my sketchbook. It's everything I ever dreamed of. *Is this what they were acting weird about all along? Am I having a prom?*

I put on the beautiful, luxurious dress — (it fits quite nicely if I do say so myself) — and walk out of my room.

I see five glittery poster board arrows taped to the wall, leading up to the front door, but I don't see anyone in the house. I then open the door to the biggest surprise ever: Ashley in a mid-length red dress, Reagan in a white blouse and black tennis skirt, and my dad in a suit. They are standing outside with a gorgeous silver Hellcat behind them.

"What is this? What's going on?"

"We made a prom for you!" says Regan.

I'm speechless. I'm not only relieved that I'm not getting kicked out, but also just stunned. *They went out of their way to create something special for me?*

Ashley walks over to me and hands me the keys. "Drive over to Fort Stanton Park. That's where the real party is," she says, clearly thrilled.

My dad just smiles and nods.

When I pull up to the park I see Rock and Richard waiting for my arrival. In front of them is a table with chicken wings, greens, mac n' cheese, cupcakes, cookies, and a cooler full of soft drinks. Over the table, silver and black balloons and streamers. Speakers play Beyonce's version of "Before I Let You Go."

"We quarantined so we can finally wrap our arms around you!" Rock yells before giving me a bear hug. It's the first time I've been in somebody's arms in a while.

"What are you guys even doing here?" I ask, not knowing what to feel.

"After we saw how broken you were on FaceTime, we reached out to your dad to come up with something to do to show that we all care," Richard responds. It's the most I've heard him say in years.

I hear this and melt, taking time to look around and soak in everything.

And that's when I see my mom and two younger brothers approach. My heart races with excitement. I didn't realize how much I needed to see them.

"You look beautiful," my mom says, with an expression on her face that says, "I've missed you." My brother Kayden looks at me and says, "Hey, Zay." "Ey Ay!" My baby brother says, trying to mimic him. Though they stay six feet away, seeing them again feels warm, natural.

When my dad and Ashley walk up, they approach the table, pick up blue Solo cups, and raise them as if they are crystal glasses. My dad clears his throat, stalling as he gathers his thoughts. "First off," he says, "It has been a tough few months, full of tension. Xzavia, I know it has been tough on you. I've seen you isolate yourself." My dad's voice starts to break. He pauses. "I'm sorry, Xzavia, for not being around more often. You deserve to feel loved. I hope you know that, no matter where I am, even if I or others are absent, we're here for you, we're on your team, and we're very aware of the amazing and crazy things that you have accomplished. Let me say clearly and loudly that

we ALL love you, Xzavia." He looks straight at me.
"Continue to shine, Zavi."

For the first time in a long time I feel chosen. I'm smiling so hard, it takes almost thirty seconds before I even realize I'm crying. For the first time, I heard my dad say the things I never believed he felt. I see my family trying and caring about me. It seems hard to believe, but... could even this cloud have a silver lining?

A RAMADAN TO REMEMBER

by Iman Ilias

Friday, April 24, 2020

I wake up to the sound of my "Illuminate" alarm at 3:30 a.m. I jolt with a start and look outside to see a pitch-black sky. I would like more than anything to pull up the covers, turn on my side, and fall into a dreamless sleep. But I have to wake up for sehri. My heart sinks as I pull off the warm blanket, and the feeling is compounded by the disappointment and anxiety I still can't seem to shake.

I splash my face with cool water to (somewhat) wake myself up and then trudge to the breakfast table. I take a seat and cup my face in my hands.

"Why has your face struck twelve?" Mama asks, lifting an omelet onto a plate.

I try to muster a smile. The long days and disrupted

nights of Ramadan take a toll on everyone, and I don't want to cause my parents any more stress than needed — especially *this* year.

"I'm fine, Mama, just completely exhausted. The first day of Ramadan, I totally forgot what this feels like," I say.

"Tell me about it," says Baba, taking a seat at the head of the table and rubbing his eyes. Danyaal and my sister Zahra peek out of their rooms and trudge towards the breakfast room as well. Kareem's still just eight, so he won't be fasting every day this month. He wants to try a practice fast on the weekend, though.

The conversation turns to a family friend of ours who was supposed to get married this summer. Mama talks with delight about how the couple met at their college's Pakistani Student Association. Her voice drops when she says, "What a shame, though, with the virus — they might have to change the date of their destination wedding in Turkey." Normally, this sort of discussion would have me completely engrossed. But today, my heart's just not in it.

So many events have been canceled. I have to imagine that the interfaith event I helped plan for Ramadan will be next. But it's too sad to accept that just yet. Everyone in the community worked so hard to put it together. I worked so hard. Since the pandemic started, though, there's been no updates on whether it will happen or not. It might be silly, but I'm still holding out hope that everything can go as planned.

My family continues on with their chatter, inexplicably

upbeat for pre-dawn. And my mother wraps her arm around me, trying to cheer me up. I love that my family's trying to get into the Ramadan spirit, and I love them for looking out for me. But I can't seem to feel excited about the holy month this year. No matter how hard I try to convince myself otherwise, it can just never be the same.

Monday, April 27, 2020

I splash my face in the sink, the cool water waking me up from a long day doing a virtual module for chemistry class. Time used to go by without me even realizing it. Now I'm conscious of every second. Screens and little boxes can never take the place of desks and real faces. I used to actually be excited about my classes, but having lessons one after the other all day really takes a lot out of you, especially when none of it is actually real. Not to mention, the sound of Mr. Stetson's soporific voice on Zoom could put someone to sleep at a heavy metal concert. I roll my sleeves up and run water over my arms, head, and ears. Lastly, I heave my feet into the sink and scrub them.

My wudu ablutions being complete, I turn off the tap and pull my headscarf over my long, tight curls. I lay my purple prayer rug with golden tassels on the carpet and begin to pray. I'm offering the midday prayer, the third of five for the day. I really need a check-in with God right now. Mama says I worry about the smallest things, and she may be right — sometimes it feels like I'm always filled with uncertainty. Insecurity about what's gonna happen later today, this week, five years down the road. That inability to feel sure of myself — and anxiety about failure — is the most undesirable emotion. I know people have different ways to deal with their fears — some journal, some use the Calm app, and some just like to breathe. But for me, prayer is my safe space. It's when I feel most productive, most calm, most heard. I know somebody's listening to what I have to say and lending me a helping hand, even if I can't see them.

I've needed this refuge of prayer more than ever since the pandemic began. It's been six weeks now since the shutdown, and it already feels like forever.

I remember the early days, when I first overheard conversations about a virus from China while walking through the hallway at school. At the time, I didn't really mind it. China was halfway across the world! I never thought it would begin to affect our life here.

Until one day in early March when Baba came rushing in, asking me to turn on the news. On-screen the Mayor of DC was holding a press conference, with the banner at the bottom reading 'Coronavirus cases rising in the DC area.'

"I'm here to provide a briefing on COVID-19 and its presence in the District of Columbia... We are confirming the District's first positive case..."

I still remember that immediate sense of doom: *What?! It's here?* My heart started to beat faster and harder in my chest. I knew this wasn't good, but still, I didn't really get it. How could I? I never could have imagined how quickly absolutely everything would change.

I clear my mind with the words that bring me comfort:
Allahumma innee audhubika inal-hammi walhazani, wal'ajzi walksali, walbukhli waljunbni, wa dhala'id-dayni a ghalabatir-rijaal.

After I finish my prayer and put my prayer rug away, I check my phone, hoping for a message from Imam Mahmoud. I texted him earlier asking if he has any updates about our interfaith event. I don't want to hear bad news, but I'm also getting too anxious not knowing anything one way or the other. Alas, my screen is blank, no new messages. It's not like Imam Mahmoud to not respond for so long. And it's strange to go so long without seeing his smiling face. We have gotten close these past few months working together; I miss him. I pretend that his silence means that he's hard at work coming up with a solution to our problem. He is so creative. I am sure he'll figure something out.

Thursday, April 30, 2020

"Resolved: The United States government ought to enact price controls on all pharmaceutical drugs," reads the resolution of this month's debate topic. We don't have normal debate competitions anymore, but they're still trying to let us do them in a virtual format. Yelling at a head in a small box on a screen isn't the same as engaging in spirited dialogue with a real live person, but I guess I'll take what I can get. Especially since we still have an hour to go until it's time to break our fasts, and I desperately need a diversion.

What would I be doing at this moment if this month was normal? I'd probably be in the mosque's tranquil garden, therapeutically stringing through my turquoise prayer beads or gazing out at the pre-sunset landscape. Little bowls of dates and water bottles would be lined up along a table at the mosque entrance, and families would slowly start driving into the parking lot for iftar...

I shake my head, trying to forget the nostalgia which now tugs at me. It's so ironic how infrequently you realize you care about something until it's taken away from you. I would give anything to go back to those quiet afternoons, meditating on the mosque garden and anticipating the delicious food I would dig into at iftar time. Back then, that was a typical Ramadan day, nothing out of the ordinary. Now, it seems like such a gift.

I'm about to doze off to the sound of Ernesto Fonesca's

rebuttal speech, so I pick up my phone, absentmindedly surfing through notifications and apps. As I scroll through my Instagram feed, I pass a poster with "Community Interfaith Event" plastered over it in big red letters. Not even registering the announcement, I scroll down until I realize what I've just read and scroll back up. "CANCELED."

The post is from the community center that was going to host our event. *Please, no. I needed this. There has to be some mistake.* It's that denial we all experience when something gut-wrenching hits us, that desire for any explanation other than the truth.

My pulse suddenly quickens, and I sit up on my bed. Having felt bored and lazy just a few seconds prior, now I'm all alert. I click on the comments below the post and read through all the disappointment. *So this is really happening,* I think. Months of effort and discussion just for this. Just to find out by clicking on an Instagram post. Without even a human voice present to let me know.

The news shatters me. After all the cancellations, you'd think that this would be just one more, but it's not. This is the final straw. Too much. I can imagine what Imam Mahmood would tell me right now — to trust that Allah will not let my hard work go to waste. Our holy book declares, "Perhaps you hate a thing, and it is good for you; and perhaps you love a thing and it is bad for you. And Allah knows, while you know not." And while I always thought I firmly believed in these teachings, all I can think about right now is my anger.

My entire body seizes up with rage. I tell myself I'm overreacting — I know others are going through far worse things at this very moment. But sometimes ration just can't beat emotion. I close my eyes and try to take a deep breath, but my heart still thunders. I slam my fist on the bed and then storm into the hallway.

"What happened to you, beta?" exclaims my father.

"They canceled it — my interfaith event!" I say, barely able to hold back tears.

"Take a deep breath, calm down, and let's talk about it," says Mama.

I take a few breaths in and out, but they're far from deep. To be honest, I don't want to calm down. I want to let my anger out, and with everything that's been happening, I think I have a right to.

"It's not fair! Iman Mahmood and I have been planning this event for almost six months now! Hundreds of people were scheduled to come! Six months of organizing, discussing, working out logistics, and now, after one second surfing through Instagram, it's all gone. It feels like this year is completely against me! Ramadan was already sucking, and now this to top it off!" I scream, all in one breath.

"Faiza," Mama says, putting her hand on my arm, "I know you are disappointed. But... let's take a step back. There are people out there who are seriously struggling right now. Have you watched the news recently? All they're showing are stories of people losing their jobs, elderly folks passing away in cramped hospitals, and children losing the opportunity to learn. This doesn't really seem like something so painful in the grand scheme of things, does it?"

Deep down, I know she's right. I know that there's so much I have to be grateful for in this crazy situation. Most importantly, I know that clearly-thinking me would try to empathize with those faring so much worse. But right now, all I can think about is my own disappointment and how unfair it is that Mama is trying to trivialize what I'm going through.

"Don't you understand?? This is all I've been looking forward to for months. I've worked so hard to make this come to life. This event was supposed to bring people from different ways of thinking together. It was supposed to be about appreciating customs outside our own. And now all of that's gone..." I say, my voice breaking mid-sentence.

By now, my siblings have also come out of their rooms to see all the commotion. Danyaal and Kareem both stare at me with wide eyes, possibly frightened. Zahra looks at me tenderly, though, and the understanding that passes between us dissipates my anger for just a second.

"Beti, I understand that the event can't take place the way you first envisioned it, but I'm sure there's still a way it can happen. Challo, have you and Imam Mahmood considered a virtual option?" Baba asks.

The thought of doing one more thing virtually, especially something so important to me, flares me up.

"No, Baba, don't you get it?! The whole point of this event was for people to be in the same space, to see each other, communicate, and connect. How can that ever happen if we're all caged in small boxes on a screen? That's the absolute last thing I would ever want to happen!"

At this point, my face is burning red. My family all looks like they're at a loss for what to do next.

"Okay, beta, I really think you need to spend some time alone right now. A little while to think about things on your own and cool off. I'll call you at iftar time," Mama says. That's code for she can't deal with me anymore.

I stand silently, hurt and slightly taken aback by her admonishment. I hurry back into my bedroom and lie down on the bed. If this were normal circumstances, I would head to the squash court and crack the ball back and forth again and again, losing my anger in the rhythm of the shots. But now, that escape is no longer possible. Courts closed, just like everything else.

I pick up my phone and tap on the Spotify app to play "Sammi Meri Waar" by Qurutulain Baloch and Umair Jaswal. It's a fast-paced version of an old South Asian wedding song, and the passion in the singers' voices and the catchy beat of the melody means it was once the perfect song to work out to. Now, I just sulk to it, shutting my eyes and pulling up the covers. I want nothing more than to forget this ever happened, and to lose myself in sleep before dinner.

🌙

When I wake up, I am feeling a little better. At least a little more like myself. I'm still disappointed, of course, and still angry. That will take some time to heal. But at least I do feel like I got some release — I had no idea how much I needed it until I actually had to explode.

I devour two helpings of Mama's qorma chawal for iftar, and then pass out on the couch. I switch on the TV and go to Netflix. Netflix has always streamed Bollywood movies, but it recently started adding a bunch of popular Pakistani dramas to its international collection. I'm just about to put on one of my all-time favorites, *Humsafar* — about a handsome, wealthy bachelor and a down-to-earth beauty thrown into an arranged marriage only to end up falling in true love — when Mama grabs the remote from me.

"Oh, come on, Faiza, we watch this one all the time. Let's try something new," she says, handing me a bowl of microwave popcorn. I glare at her, but she does know the way to my heart: popcorn. And also, rom-coms. She drifts through our DVR recordings and selects one of my favorites, *The Devil Wears Prada*.

I stuff a fistful of popcorn into my mouth as Anne Hathaway does her morning routine to "Suddenly I See." I always did love this opening.

Mama looks my way lovingly, almost cautiously.

"What?" I say.

She takes my hand in hers. "I know you are having a very hard time right now, beta. The last thing I want to do is make you feel worse, but…"

"What's wrong?" I say, sitting up.

"Well, I got a phone call from my friend at the mosque this afternoon, and it turns out Iman Mahmood has been sick, and he just tested positive for COVID..."

My heart drops.

"I know you're probably scared for him, but remember, one of the most important things he's taught you is to never give up on your faith, even when things look horrible."

The news hits me like a school bus. I honestly don't even know what to think, and I try not to. I know that if I really allow myself to process this, I might spiral down into a place I don't want to go right now.

"How is he?" I ask.

"He's with his family, for now. He's in good hands. And if he needs it, there are talented doctors at our hospital..." Mama trails off and I can tell she's worried, too. I know not to ask any more right now.

I sit there, frozen. *This is why he didn't text me back.* Mama puts a hand on my shoulder.

"Hey, I know these past couple of weeks have been a roller coaster. But we can always find ways to feel better, right? Like watching a feel-good movie on the couch, and eating junk food, together?"

I nod, and lean into her. She's right — it's the little things that have been helping me through. Small comforts that let us make sense out of a world that doesn't make any sense.

Later that night, after finishing Isha prayer, I cup my hands and make a personal prayer to God. I pray that the effects of this pandemic are only temporary. That all the people who are suffering have their pain alleviated. That the father who can no longer support his children finds a job again. That the children who are stuck at home can soon go back to school. I pray that my dear Imam Mahmood recovers as quickly as possible, and is giving a sermon at the mosque again in no time. I pray that even though he is weakened right now, and his body fatigued, he can get back to being the lively, always-smiling man that I know. And as hard as it is, I thank God for the perspective that Imam's illness brings. I feel so foolish, having broken down just hours ago about our event being canceled. It seems like a minuscule issue now. If there is one thing this wild time is teaching me, it's that most concerns are actually small. And the people you love, they are what truly matter.

Friday, May 1, 2020

The next day at iftar, Mama takes out a new box of jumbo Medjool dates and sets a tall jug of cherry-red Rooh Afza on the table. Rooh Afza is the "summer drink of the East," as all containers with Rooh Afza syrup read. Some people don't see the appeal, but I personally think it's the most refreshing beverage ever made. It's cool, but not icy cold, and it's sweet but not too saccharine. What I love most about it is the hint of rose you can taste right at the end of a gulp. I used to drink it with Imam Mahmoud, and I wonder if Mama knows this, if she served it as a kind of offering. I can't get him out of my mind.

As I watch the red syrup swirl in the liquid, I remember the first time he and I shared this drink together, at the mosque a few years ago. I was feeling really down at the time, and he noticed immediately, as he always did.

"Drink something," he said, extending a cold glass of Rooh Afza towards me. "You've been dehydrated all day, and Maghrib salah is about to start."

I took the glass absentmindedly and continued staring into a corner.

"Muslim Student Association meeting not go well?" he asked.

I sighed dramatically. "Can you call it a meeting when nobody else shows up?"

Imam Mahmood chuckled. "Do not fret so much, dear Faiza. I'm proud of you for working to create this

73

important group. I have faith that it will come together."

"Really?" I asked. I was beginning to think it was hopeless.

"Oh, of course! Back when I was in high school, I tried to start a group of my own — a sci-fi book club. But when I asked friends to join, they laughed out loud. 'Be part of a science fiction book club? What, and look like geeks in front of the entire school?' I knew for a fact that many of them were die-hard sci-fi fans in secret, but they didn't want to admit it in public, in case other kids thought they weren't 'cool' anymore."

"And so what happened?" I asked. It was kind of amusing — and reassuring? — to think of this history repeating itself.

"Oh, I still went ahead and ran the club. It was never super popular, but by the time I graduated, I had assembled a small group of fellow sci-fi enthusiasts to talk about books and watch movies with. And when I left, one of my juniors became the new president and continued to run the club as a haven for future sci-fi nerds at our school. And that's exactly what you're doing. Creating a haven, a safe space for Muslim students at your school that's going to last for years to come."

I smiled.

"That is exactly what I'm trying to do, Imam, but sometimes it feels like it's all for nothing."

"Like Allah says in the Quran, 'Everyone is rewarded for the effort one makes.' You may just not be seeing that reward right now."

I smile again now at the sweet memory. Imam Mahmood has such a calming presence, and he uses advice from our religion so artfully to make me feel better. Not many people in this world can truly understand all my intricacies, but he is one of them. I can't imagine losing him, and just the thought of it makes my stomach knot. Why did *he*, of all people, have to get this terrible virus?

So many things have been turned on their head this year. Imam Mahmood getting COVID is just another sign of how much our world has shifted. His getting sick almost confirms that nothing can go back to normal ever again.

Monday, May 4, 2020

As I sit trying to leaf through our latest assigned poem for Spanish Lit, "Hombres necios," my phone suddenly pings with a new notification. It's from WhatsApp. Ayesha, a young woman who goes to our mosque, has created a new group chat called "Help for Imam Mahmood."

I open the group to see she has added almost all of the regular attendants at our congregation. A message suddenly appears in the empty thread.

Ayesha

> AssalamuAlaikum everybody. I think many of you already know that Imam Mahmood was diagnosed with COVID-19 this week and is currently in quarantine. He's still quite sick, but we pray for his healing. I wanted to create this chat so that we can all coordinate ways to help. I'm keeping in touch with his family for info on anything they need – Ayesha

I smile at the message. This is such a sweet thing for Ayesha to do. I wonder what I can do to help.

As I'm contemplating ideas, my phone suddenly pings with more and more messages.

Zaynab

Thank you so much for this, Ayesha. I'm going to text Farhana right now, letting her know that I'm bringing by some daal chawal for dinner.

Fareeda Aunty

AssalamuAlaikum, I'll be sending my son over with some chicken corn soup and baklava.

Bilal Uncle

Does Imam Mahmood need any more medicines? I'd be happy to run over to CVS and pick up anything for him.

Ibrahim Bhai

I'm at the Giant right now, and I can pick up any supplies needed, whether it be masks, sanitizer wipes, or food.

My heart warms at seeing how passionate our community is about helping the Imam, and how it only took one little message for everyone to come out to support him. It's definitely a testament to what an amazing person Imam Mahmood is, and to me, it also represents how unique our community is.

I rush outside to ask Mama what we can drop off at Imam Mahmood's house.

"I thought that answer would be quite obvious for you," she says with a knowing smile. "Why don't you do your favorite?"

She's right — I completely forgot about our favorite recipe. Imam Mahmood and I both love chicken karahi, a rich curry filled with spices and green peppers. I don't know if he can eat it just yet, but won't it be a great first meal when he's feeling well again?

I'm a hopeless cook, so I ask Mama for help. I've always thought it's amazing how easily she makes these complicated, delicious meals, but when I start cooking, I realize it's not quite as hard as it seems. When the karahi is finally ready, Mama and I put it in a tray and drive over to Imam Mahmood's house. My heart tugs at me as I walk up the driveway, wondering what's going on inside and how he must be feeling. I set the tray down at his front door with a Get Well Soon note.

Just then, I see two more cars pull up. Even with masks on, I can still make out the familiar faces from the mosque taking trays of food and medicine packets out of their trunks. As they walk up the driveway and I head back to the car, we exchange friendly waves and salaams.

The funny thing is, at that moment, I feel like even though we can't be physically together anymore, we're still just as much there for each other as always.

Wednesday, May 13, 2020

Zahra and I lay out the prayer rugs, calling everyone to pray Maghrib. After breaking our fast with dates each night at dusk, we offer Maghrib prayer before sitting down to dig into the proper meal. My siblings and I are always eager to get through prayer quickly so that we can eat the delicious food Mama has prepared. We're now entering the last ten nights of Ramadan, the most holy. It's the time when prayers are sure to be answered, and forgiveness for our past mistakes should be made. The mosque is usually jam-packed during the last ten days, and people stay up all night there praying.

When we finish Maghrib and sit down at the dinner table to eat, Baba tells us, "Brother Ramy from the mosque is setting up a virtual prayer circle. We're supposed to log into Zoom after Isha prayer. He emailed a list of surahs he'd like to go over."

The news slightly takes me aback, even though we've been doing so many activities virtually lately. I'm so used to going to the congregation building and gathering in circles on the floor to read the Quran or recite small prayers. The idea of congregating virtually is odd, but at the same time, I think it's a really nice idea considering that it gives us a way to meet even in these crazy circumstances. Also it gives us a chance as a community to come together and pray for Imam's continued recovery. It's been two weeks now since he was diagnosed, and though he never had to go to the hospital — Alhamdulillah — his progress towards healing is quite slow. We are all impatient for him to be well again, but are trusting that he is on that path.

We all gather in front of the computer with our Qurans. As we log in, we see more and more people joining the room. I giggle as I see some of the older aunties and uncles trying to turn their cameras on. After greeting each other, Brother Ramy asks us to open to the 29th chapter of the Quran. We all take turns unmuting and reciting portions of the chapter. Even though we're all in different rooms, maybe even in completely different parts of the city, it feels like we really are all reading together in the same space.

My heart feels warm, and for the first time in a while, my mind feels occupied with more than just sifting through upsetting thoughts of how isolated and bored I feel. Reading the Quran again, I realize it's been a long time since I really opened it up and reflected on its meaning. I forgot how doing so grounds me and makes the world's chaos seem a little clearer. While I've been focusing so much on how nothing is the same, I didn't realize that my belief is one thing that is and always will be constant.

Brother Ramy announces that we'll be holding these virtual congregations every night for the rest of Ramadan. I am surprised by how much comfort the idea brings me. I thought this would be like yet another Zoom event, but it actually means so much more than that. I am grateful, and I cannot wait until Imam can join us.

Sunday, May 24, 2020

When I wake up on Eid morning, the sun is shining extra bright. I smile. Maybe nobody's celebrating Eid the same way today, but nature hasn't forgotten what day it is. I walk to the kitchen in my pajamas. It seems I'm the last person in the house to get up today, because my entire family shouts "Eid Mubarak!" as I enter the room. I laugh and wish them the same. "Merry Christmas," "Shabbat Shalom," "Eid Mubarak," — there are some greetings in every religion which automatically lift your spirits and make the day special.

On the table I see my favorite breakfast — halwa puri, deep-fried bread and confectionate sweetmeat (essentially a heart attack on a plate.) And next to that, I see a box of assorted Dunkin' Donuts Munchkins. As much of a desi girl as I am, there's no way I can resist a powdered Munchkin. I rush over to the box and take one out.

On her laptop, Mama signs into the Zoom link that the mosque sent for the virtual Eid congregation. The first face we see when we log in is Imam Mahmood, a bit thinner but smiling widely. My heart lifts. I'm so relieved to see him! He's shooting his usual ear-to-ear smile, which makes it feel like everything's going to be okay. I spent so much time imagining what he must look like in his condition, and this image soothes me more than I can say.

"It's so nice to see everyone, albeit in such a different way," Imam Mahmood chuckles. "Thank you everyone

for your heartfelt concern. Alhamdulillah I'm on the road
to recovery and feeling a lot stronger. I could never have
gotten to this point without all your help."

The chat blows up with people welcoming Imam
Mahmood and asking him how he's doing. It's clear how
beloved he is among us — we were all so worried. We all
feast on Munchkins and halwa puri as we hear him deliver
his first sermon since falling ill.

"Of course, we can't celebrate Eid the same way today,
and so many of the things we look forward to doing every
year aren't possible. But that doesn't take away the need
to acknowledge the importance of this day. This is a day
to celebrate our accomplishments over the last month. To
thank God for giving us the ability to enjoy our blessings
today. And to be proud of being part of the Muslim
ummah. So even if you can't enjoy the company of friends
in person today, do something, any little thing, to make
this day special."

Our family has already organized a plan for Eid.
Mama picked up a bunch of boxes of mithai from the
Pakistani store last weekend and we all helped her wrap
them in nice wrapping paper and ribbons. The plan is
to drive around the city today giving each of our friends
a box of sweets and greeting them for Eid (in a socially-
distanced way, of course).

After breakfast, we all shuffle into our rooms to get
dressed. On normal Eids, we get decked out in our fanciest
embroidered clothes, and I get my hair straightened and

wear my newest jewelry. But this year, obviously, will be different. We can't wear our nicest clothes and drive around in our Honda all day. It's another custom that's changed that I hadn't even thought about before. Now that I do, though, it hurts a little.

I find a simple blue kurta, or Pakistani tunic, with little yellow flowers embroidered all over it. This is perfect. Not as fancy as usual but nice. Just like Imam Mahmood said: finding a way to celebrate this day, even if it's not how we ordinarily would.

On the drive to our first stop, Baba says "Takbeer" and we all respond "AllahuAkbar." This is a tradition Muslim families are supposed to do every Eid on the way to morning prayer. AllahuAkbar is the Arabic phrase for "God is Great." Even though we're not driving towards the mosque right now, it just feels right.

At each stop, we leave our treats at their front door, then ring their doorbell and retreat to a safe distance. We wait, in hopes of connecting. The reactions we get at every house pleasantly surprise me. People who I usually know to be reserved are chirpy, eager to catch up. It's a reminder of how we have all begun to crave human connection after weeks of separation. It seems like everyone is very pleasantly surprised to have their unconventional Eid day interrupted by our visit. We spend as much time as possible talking to everyone, finding out someone is graduating or someone just got engaged. People tell us how their Ramadan has been and we share the same.

It seems like even though our world has shifted, the friendships we have with these people have remained exactly the same. In fact, given the fact that we realize how much we need each other, our connections seem to have deepened.

I watch the boxes of packaged sweets disappear one by one from our trunk as we make the rounds around the entire Northwest part of the city — from Chevy Chase where we live, across Rock Creek Park over to Takoma, and then way down to Woodley Park, near the Islamic Center of DC. As we finally drop the last box off and start the drive back home, I feel humbled and amazed — for all the ways we have tried to make the impossible possible, to stay separate, but never apart. And now I have just one more thing to do, to close out Eid in the best way I know how...

After adjusting my hair in the reflection of my dark computer screen and making sure there aren't any creases in my shirt, I take a deep breath and click on the Zoom link Imam Mahmood sent me. It's actually happening: our interfaith event! As the white waiting-room screen shifts and I'm accepted into the meeting, I'm stunned by the flood of smiling faces. I watch as more and more of them fill up my monitor, and I'm moved by so many people coming together in this moment to learn from each other.

I know I said that "the last thing I could possibly want was a virtual interfaith event," but, well, here we are. And I'm nothing but excited. Before all this started, I had this very specific, idealistic view of how this event should play out for it to be a success. And honestly, that's how I felt about most things in my life. But given everything we've gone through these past few months, I realize that not everything has to be exactly like I pictured it. In fact, it can't be. And despite all the sadness and anxiety and heartache and hurt this pandemic has brought, the values I believe in and the people I care about are things I can hold on to no matter what else changes. I can choose to lean into one true thing: I am growing. I am changing. And I'm stronger than I imagined. We all are.

"Welcome!" I say into my camera. "We are SO glad you are here."

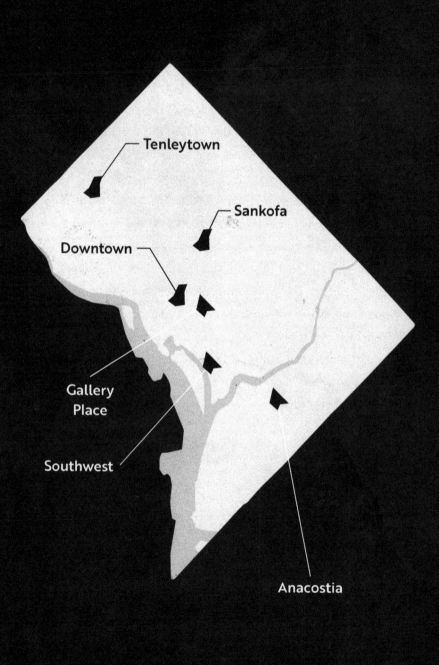

SUMMER

BORN IN BLACK

by Camal Shorter

Sunday, May 24, 2020

You can always tell it's him coming down the stairs when you hear the noise that the chair lift makes. It's the same sound I hear early in the morning, before the sun decides to show its face. It's inconvenient, but it's pretty impressive how active the guy is, given his disposition.

Me and Ma Ma (Carretta to you) were already seated at the breakfast table enjoying the very soothing voice of Ray Charles through the antique record player cabinet. I've been trying to introduce these two to Bluetooth since I got here, but that's been a tree that refuses to bear fruit. I call him Pop Pop, but to you, he'll be Earl, and when he rolled in he spoke at an obnoxious volume.

Earl: There I was, my Walkman in my lap and headgear over my ears. It was just me, the wind, the road, and Otis Redding. I was flying, baby. You should've seen me. I got to the top of that hill and I just... I don't know, I felt young again. I was fearless!

I noticed that he seemed to be hiding his left hand.

Carretta: You said you got to the top of the hill?

She seemed amused.

Earl: I did.

Carretta: How'd you get there?

Earl: I pushed myself up.

She seemed disappointed. She only said his name and she said it with two extra L's.

Carretta: Earlll!

Earl: Fine, baby, I fell.

Carretta: Earl, that's twice now. Pretty soon I'll have to start joining you.

Earl: I don't want you going through the trouble. You got a nice routine going with your whole yoga thing you've been doing.

Carretta: Earl, honey what if you fall and can't get up?

Earl: I'll pull myself up by my teeth if I have to! If I let this wheelchair deter me from having fun then I'll be old and grumpy and you won't love loving me no more. I won't be a burden, nor a chore.

Carretta reached for his hand, held it there and smiled.

Carretta: So you gonna let me take a look at your arm here?

She continued by examining his arm.

Earl: Nothing to worry about. It was a gentle fall.

Carretta: Doesn't look gentle. Your arm's all scratched up.

Earl: I'm fine, baby. Don't worry yourself.

Carretta: I know you're resilient so you'll be okay, but you need to clean this.

He seemed to just stare for a moment before he hit a U-turn in his wheelchair. Carretta grabbed the back of his shoulder.

Carretta: Hey, Earl, who helped you get up?

Her hands were on his cheek now.

Earl: *(with a chuckle)* Oh it was a white boy, about Roman's age.

Carretta: And were you nice?

Earl: Nice? I should've ran him over! You don't go 'round touching old folk with your nasty teenage COVID hands.

He did all this as he rolled off to find the alcohol wipes in the cabinet under the bathroom sink. Ma Ma gave him a stern look and went about eating her meal.

Carretta: So Roman, how's everything? It's been a year now.

She could've asked me about school, but instead, she asked me about the one-year anniversary of the crash. I raised my spoon and my head, and only after I placed the drawstring from my hoodie into my mouth did I speak.

Roman: You mean how's everything since my parents died?

Death itself had entered the room and the air grew pale. After letting the awkwardness play out, I began my next words with a smirk.

Roman: But no, I'm fine. It's fine. I miss living in Chicago, but at least I now have something great to talk about for my college essays. They'll eat my orphan story right up.

She seemed tense and I thought that that might have been a bit prick-ish of me, but she's pretty familiar with how I use humor to mask how I really feel. Then she leaned into me when she said this:

Carretta: Oh Roman, you're a lot like your father, you know. You're so brave and are just as intelligent as you are hard-headed, and I'll tell you just like I used to have to tell him.

(with an emphasis on my name she goes)

Like water, Roman, emotions need somewhere to go.

She of course said something I was thankful to hear, but

sometimes she loved preaching too much. I should be fair to her though and give some context. She hadn't taught since retirement, so having an adolescent around must trigger an instinct to educate.

Earl rolled in, parked at the kitchen table, and placed his arm on display at the breakfast table.

Earl: Hey, Carretta, will you wrap my arm up, please?

I never seen him smile so wide.

Carretta: Sure, Earl.

Earl: Hey, Roman, have I ever told you how I met my guardian angel?

Carretta: Aww, Earl, after all these years you're still so sweet on me?

Roman: Huh, I'm not sure I heard this one.

Earl: It was December 3, 1969. I had just got my fro big enough to hold my afro pick.

He must've just found his pick in the bathroom because he waved it at me. There was a Black Power fist at the base of it.

I used to play my saxophone in the streets to earn some extra cash in my free time. On this day the night began to creep in, and I had just finished up. Right before I could take Betty off my neck, I heard the most soothing and mellifluous voice. It said to me, "Got time for one more?"

Carretta: And he said, "For you, I do." And he played me a seductive tune.

Roman: Yeah, that part you didn't have to share.

Earl: Stay outta grown folk business. Anyway, I felt lucky so I invited her to join me at the Golden Peacock. She put a spell on me. I don't know what got into me. I'd have never abandoned my duty as a Panther if I hadn't met your grandmother that beautiful fateful day. You see, Roman, I'd have otherwise been in that apartment with my Chairman, Fred Hampton. You see, the government wanted him dead. He was growing too influential, too fast, too young. He was able to unite working class poor people of all races and formed a "Rainbow Coalition." It was a struggle against classism. It was a dangerous struggle. In fact, the director of the FBI at the time referred to the Black Panther Party as the greatest threat to the internal security of America. They killed Fred Hampton! And if it wasn't for this wonderful, winsome, charming and charismatic young lady here they'd have got me too!

Knock, knock, knock.

Earl: Now who the hell is that?

Roman: Oh, that's Jackson. We're about to go hit the cages.

Earl raised an eyebrow as if he was The Rock himself.

Earl: That lil' white boy?

I saw Ma Ma's face before she said it. She cast Earl's name as if it were a spell.

Carretta: Earl!

Woof. She judged him, she called his name.

Earl: You know his father's a racist cop. He's a white supremacist!

Ma Ma knew better than to get him started. We both did.

Earl: Listen here, grandson. You beware that boy. I know how cool they can seem, especially these progressive young types, but I know firsthand *(said slowly and emphatically)* THEY WILL LET YOU DOWN. Now, go have fun.

Roman: *(with a harmonious chuckle that carried throughout his voice)* Oh-kay.

Carretta: Hey, Roman.

Roman: Yes, Ma Ma?

Carretta: I almost forgot! I stopped at Sankofa the other day and saw this! You remember Baldwin, right?

Roman: Vaguely.

She handed me a book. On the cover, there was a black and white picture from the olden days of a man looking pensive. The Fire Next Time, it read.

I told her that I had to go, but I remembered to tell her

"thank you" just before I opened the door to slip out. I was going to close the door behind me, but she stayed there in the frame.

Carretta: Hey, Jackson, how are you?

Jackson: I'm fine and you?

Carretta: I'm doing just fine, baby.

Earl: *(in a harrowing howl)* Don't you bring that snowflake into our home!

I turned to Jackson. He didn't seem pleased. I wasn't too pleased either, but I was in a position where it was better to just laugh it off.

Roman: Ha ha.

Carretta: Don't you mind him. You two go on and have fun.

Though it was faint, I could hear Ma Ma fussing at Earl as she shut the door.

Carretta: You have to stop doing that! That's your grandson's friend!

Jackson and I made our way to the cages.

Jackson: What was that about?

Roman: What's what about?

Jackson: Your grandfather. I helped the guy up after he fell and he pretended that he didn't know me, and just now he called me "snowflake" and said I wouldn't be allowed in…

Roman: He probably didn't recognize you behind your mask. And, as for the whole "snowflake" thing… he was joking… mostly.

Jackson: Mostly? What the hell does that mean?

Roman: Your dad.

Jackson: Yeah, my dad's a dick.

Roman: You see, my grand pop, he's been called 'boy,' 'nigger,' 'spear chucker,' all those racist things. The problem isn't necessarily *who* you are, it's *what* you are.

I gave an unfortunate smile.

Jackson: So I'm racist because I'm white.

Roman:

But before I could say "yes but no"…

Jackson: So where do we go from this? Just shame all white people?

Roman: Well, I know it is much easier to point the finger when you're not the one on the runway. But you should understand that my great-grandfather was a sharecropper, and my grandfather Earl and his siblings picked tobacco and cotton as kids. Then he went off and fought a war for this country and they still treated him like dirt when he got back. He faced a world that told him every day and to his face that he was not allowed in, that he could not drink here or use the bathroom there. Every day when he walked outside he was reminded of his place. "Why?" he asked… and no one answered.

Jackson: Okay, yeah, of course, but none of that is on me. I mean, I helped the man up when he fell. What am I guilty of? My only crime against your grandfather has been the color of my skin. I know I can't like call myself a 'victim of racism' or whatever, but by definition your grandfather's a racist, right? And if that's tolerable from him but not from me, where are we going as a planet of people?

Roman: I hear you. You're not guilty. But you're not innocent either. You should understand that my grandfather is well within reason to be spiteful. The world has done something to him and that world was white. Racism is not an individual pursuit. It's like a series of vines. Picture an abandoned house somewhere where nature has consumed it, and it's just everywhere.

Jackson: What has racism done to you? Not your grandfather, not to Black people as a whole, but you.

Roman: I have no idea.

I lied. It was too much of a chore having to validate being oppressed.

Jackson: Exactly!

Roman: What are you exact-ing about?

Jackson: There must be another side to this.

We reached the batting cages and went to pick out our bats. A moment went by. We were due for a new subject, so I changed the topic.

Roman: If a genie gave you the chance to be any other animal in the world, what would you be?

Jackson: Kangaroo.

Roman: What, bro?

Jackson puffed up his chest and brought his two fists down to his waist, making a muscular oval with his arms. And then, man, I kid you not, he started hopping.

Jackson: Kangaroos have the muscle to kick a force of over like 700 pounds! Look at me, I'm jacked too! That's why they named me Jackson. I came out the belly Jacked.

I laughed my ass off.

Jackson: What would you be?

Roman: Octopus!

Jackson did an almost-laugh.

Jackson: Why?

Roman: I'm just so goddamn efficient, and like an octopus, what can't I do?

We both found it funny, and suddenly we grew silent as the first ball came in.

(thwack)

Monday evening, May 25, 2020

Only humans have to do homework. Also, it's silly, but think about it: only humans have to go and find a bathroom to use before they can pee. It hit me: I go to school to go to work.

Roman: Ma Ma! Ma Ma!

I yelled as I fought my way down the steps.

Carretta sat patiently at the piano. Her last finger lifted off of middle C and her melody came to an unintended stop.

Roman: Listen to this: I go to school to go to work.

Carretta gave a polite smile.

Carretta: Roman, what does this mean?

Roman: You also went to school to go to work.

Carretta: And what does that mean?

Roman: My son will go to school to go to work.

I grabbed my phone because it summoned me.

Carretta: That phone you love, someone went to school to go to work to build that.

I walked away and sat back down at my computer before I was summoned once again. This time a phone call. "RNP" by Cordae featuring Anderson .Paak began to play — naturally, I let it ring...

…but eventually, I answered the phone.

Jackson: Heyyy, mann. How's it going?

He sounded like he needed to get something out.

Roman: Why do you sound like that time on Halloween when you had to run to the bushes after you ate too many Harry Potter jelly beans?

He must've thought it was funny because the laughter carried throughout his sentence with a hum, but as if he had no intention to laugh.

Jackson: pffffffff what?! Man, I thought we agreed that what happened on Halloween STAYS in Halloween.

His laughter was contagious. But he let it taper off…

Jackson: So you haven't seen the video?

Roman: What?

Jackson: Dude it's all over Instagram, Twitter, how have you not seen it?

Roman: I've been cramming trying to get a head start on this essay.

Jackson: I told you not to take AP.

Roman: Yeah, well I can't afford to be mediocre.

Jackson: Roman, just check social media. And I'll talk to you later.

Roman: Whatever. See you.

*I still had work to do, so I didn't check social media.
Not yet.*

Tuesday morning, May 26, 2020

It was morning now, and breakfast was over. I decided to sit with Ma Ma and Pop Pop in the living room and watch the news until I had to be on-camera for school.

"Protests break out throughout the city of Minneapolis due to yet another killing of an unarmed Black man. George Floyd was said to have clearly stated multiple times that he could not breathe, and the officers continued to kneel on his neck. Here, folks, is the very shocking footage gathered from the scene."

This must have been the video Jackson meant. I watched in silence.

It was… hard to watch.

I wondered what exactly frightened the officer. Was his skin too aggressive? Was his demeanor resistant? Why was his knee on his neck? Were the handcuffs not enough? What warranted his behavior towards George? Was he too big, too Black? Why do we get treated this way?

Earl: They got another one of us.

Earl's knuckles whitened as he clenched the rubber of his wheelchair, unintentionally jerking himself forward.

Ma Ma stared at her husband. If her look were verbal it would have uttered a phrase of disappointment. But she already knew that his glibness came from pain.

Roman: Sheesh. But… he's got a point. I mean as long as I've been alive there's been a death and a protest and rants about police brutality and what's not being done for us and people pretend to change then that dies down until one of us "gets got" again and then Black Lives Matter again. Well, until Black History Month, then every commercial has a dashiki in it. You can't help but… be numb sometimes.

Earl: You see in my time, we had Jim Crow. We knew who sent him, we knew who sicked the dogs on us, we knew who the enemy was. After the Civil Rights Act, Jim went underground so you couldn't see him. He adapted and hid behind words like "inclusion" and "progress." Dr. King, with all he accomplished before he was assassinated, said that he felt like he was integrating us into a burning house, and he was speaking to you, Roman, when he said this. "Let us become firemen; we won't stand by and let the house burn."

Then Ma Ma said something next. She said something about choosing my battles and not responding to oppression in a way that kept white people comfortable. I just nodded my head. Not because I didn't take her words seriously, it was just that her voice got pushed to the background, behind my own thoughts. I was stuck on what Pop Pop said. Talking about Jim Crow and progress and inclusion. Talking about Jim Crow went underground like he's the goddamned boogeyman.

*I don't understand this. Why was there a nigger in the
first place? I realized I must've said it out loud because
Ma Ma asked, "What was that, Roman?"*

I continued as if I was asking the room.

Roman: Yeah, sometimes I just think. About the n-word.
About its use and I think why. Why was there ever one in
the first place?

*Ma Ma seemed impressed by the depth of my question,
and Earl spoke up immediately with an answer.*

Earl: They had to justify all the wrong they do.

*He leaned forward in his chair. A story was coming, you
could tell.*

I served with a soldier named Sherman Odecky.

Carretta: Earl, you need to let that go.

She must've heard it so many times.

Earl: Nah, the boy needs to hear this. I saved that ungrateful
bastard's life. He would've died if I didn't shoot that
soldier off of him in Vietnam. After that, we were the best
of friends, brothers even. But when we returned home to
America, he stopped taking my calls. Even passed him on
the street once, I saw the recognition in his eyes, and yet
he said nothin'! Just walked past me like I was nothin'!

*I had heard this story before too, he just didn't remember.
There may be no story more formative to Pop Pop than*

this one, and I knew it well. I looked at my phone —
8:29 a.m. I had to go to class.

Roman: I hear you, Pop Pop. And I've heard it before. I
just don't wanna be late for class.

The old man shook his head and I went upstairs to Zoom
into homeroom.

Ms. Frantner was (as Pop Pop would put it) a "young
progressive." She started her first job and taught during
COVID all in the same year. She taught world history
but I only had her for homeroom, and homeroom was
nice because you didn't have to be on-camera.

But *she* was on camera, and she looked shaken.

Ms. Frantner: Good morning, class. I just want to
say right off the bat that something terrible happened
yesterday, and I want to make space for discussion… I
think it's especially important that we *listen* right now.

Here we go, I thought.

Roman.

She paused awkwardly.

Now more than ever, your voice is important, and if you're
willing, I think your perspective is something the class
should hear.

Being the only Black kid in class was NOT fun. Exhibit A.

Roman: Well, Ms. Frantner, I think race is a complex and very multifaceted thing. A thing I can't really comprehend. It seems to be a social and economic hierarchy, and people who look like me don't seem to be on top.

She said nothing. This didn't seem to be what she expected. I picked up the silence.

Roman: What happened to George Floyd makes my blood boil. And it makes me angry to hear folks act like it's an outlier. It makes me question the validity of non-violence. And it is very easy for me to feel this way. Especially when born in Black.

Some people — the teacher's pets, mostly — were on-camera, and you could see them shift in their seats.

Ms. Frantner: Could you maybe elaborate? What makes you feel this way?

Roman: History tells us who we are and, as Foundational Blacks, our history begins in captivity — as if we evolved into slaves. How do you garner a sense of pride when you've been ⅗ths a person and a ni—

Before I could even get to the 'g,' I felt the classroom tense. Marge rolled her eyes. Hunter's face went blank. Some of the cameras turned off altogether. I shifted gears.

Roman: Like why do white people seem to have more? Surely, there's nothing inherently special about white children.

Ms. Frantner: Well, no. There is not.

And although she smiled, her face seemed to be let down. This was not what she wanted to hear from me. What did she want? Something she could nod along to, and feel like she was "one of the good ones"? But she listened. The kids in the chat were listening too.

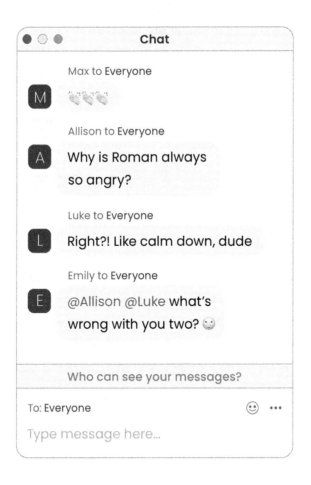

Seeing my classmates talk about me like I asked to be put on this podium… it was just ridiculous. I was so tired of tiptoeing around transgressions. I didn't want to be nice about this. I wanted to be specific, name it, call it out. The class shouldn't be kept comfortable — I knew I wasn't. So then I just let it all out.

Roman: In this country, it has been people who look like you who cracked the whip, who sicked the dogs, tied the noose, who knelt on the neck, or who watched and did nothing. Someone has to be billed for my grandmother's tears. And today, even when you and people who look like you still benefit from that agony, it was YOU who singled me out to be the spokesperson on Black death.

I said this and it was as if time itself needed a moment. The chat went still. The remaining cameras turned off. Ms. Frantner looked stunned. She slow-blinked and then nodded her head.

Ms. Frantner: …Okay. Roman. That was… But you are right — I should not have put you on the spot. I think… I think no one knows just how to react in these situations. I know I don't. I think we're trying our best. *I'm* trying my best. It's… We have a long way to go.

She sighed a huge sigh and then reacted to a ding on her computer.

And I hate to cut short this important discussion but I just got word that we are moving to classes early today, so homeroom is over. Class, stay safe, and… uh… Roman, we will continue this conversation. See you all next time.

My door was usually closed, but there was Ma Ma standing there in between the door frame.

Carretta: What class was it that you just finished with?

Roman: Oh that was homeroom.

I wondered if she'd heard me. She probably had something to say about the 'importance of respecting my teachers,' but I went on…

Ms. Frantner told me my voice was important and that my perspective was something the class should hear.

Carretta: I see.

She smiled and turned to leave. But it was a sad smile, so she might have heard the whole thing after all. And that was fine by me.

9:30

F Four Minneapolis Cops Fired After
Shocking Video Goes Viral

May 26, 2020

U U.S. Coronavirus death toll reaches
100,000

May 27, 2020

C Chaotic scene in Minneapolis after
second night of protests

May 28, 2020

D Demonstrators in DC Gather to
Protest Death of George Floyd

May 29, 2020

Swipe to unlock

Friday evening, May 29, 2020

*The next few days were spent going back and forth
between my Zoom classes and the TV. My teachers were
"trying to be sensitive," and the news was filled with
Black Lives Matter demonstrations. I felt scattered.
And now that the school year had officially ended this
afternoon, I was in front of the news again with Ma Ma,
watching our country's rage at the death of a Black man.
What a way to start the summer...*

Carretta: I thought school ended this afternoon. What
you over there working on?

*She gestured to me from the sofa as I sat at the table with
a pack of old markers and some cardboard.*

Roman: Oh, this isn't for school, Ma Ma.

Carretta: I hear you and your granddad are going
downtown tomorrow for the protest, is this true?

Roman: Yeah, we're taking the train.

Carretta: Alright, Roman.

*Her face seemed to say that she made herself okay with it
but then she seemed curious... worried even.*

Carretta: Why are you protesting tomorrow?

*Without saying I word, I picked up the cardboard and I
showed her the sign I made.*

Carretta: "Wealth is in each other."

She smiled and nodded.

Saturday, May 30, 2020

"I can't breathe"

"I can't breathe"

"I can't breathe"

We had just arrived. It was hot. I almost bought a Black Lives Matter towel to wipe the sweat from my forehead and to shade me from the sun. I decided I didn't need it. Using my shirt would suffice. I'd save my money. It was too loud to think. All the commotion, all the anger and shouting started to have its influence on me. I felt myself getting agitated… I just didn't understand why Pop Pop wouldn't get an electric wheelchair! It just made no sense for me to push my legs like this when he could easily push a lever forward instead, so I told him.

Roman: You need to get one of those electric ones so I don't have to push you around like this.

Earl: What happens when the battery goes out?

Roman: You'll charge it.

Earl chuckled.

Earl: You know it's about time I got an upgrade. I done had this wheelchair since before you was born. Hey, look at that, that looks like a good spot.

This time he pushed his own wheels and we moved over to where the crowd was gathered. On our way over there he told me he was going to wait for the right moment of silence.

Protester dude: NO JUSTICE!

Protesters: NO PEACE!

Protester dude: NO BRUTAL!

Protesters: POLICE!

When the chanting stopped, Earl grabbed a megaphone. And in his very old yet mellifluous voice he preached while I swayed my sign that said WEALTH IS IN EACH OTHER.

Earl: I see "Black Lives Matter" t-shirts being sold and I think, *Damn that's cool, young comrades supporting one another.* And then I think, *What's next?* What's next, Black people? After selling t-shirts, build schools. After selling t-shirts, buy housing. Invest in Black businesses. Teach group economics. Become self-reliant! The wealth is in each other!

And he rolled off. I imagine that to him that line was like a fatality in Mortal Kombat. Knock-Out.

Suddenly two 20-something-year-olds came up to Earl. One had a camera and the other was "The Personality." They asked if it was okay to ask him a couple questions and he said he didn't mind.

I sat where I stood and I watched and I listened. They

learned that Earl was a Panther and a Vietnam vet, and then they asked him about race relations and whether or not he thought true equality could happen. Their questions were the perfect opening to get him to tell the Odecky story... again. Which he did. Then he wrapped with some parting wisdom.

Earl: So I say that to say this: Maintaining the status quo stifles change. Black Americans have been at war and have been fighting the same fight since our arrival. I think true change will happen because it has to. I just don't think I'll live to see it, and I'm not so sure my grandson will either, but his son should see it. There's just so much more progress to be made.

The camera dude and The Personality thanked us and left.

All of a sudden, off to the side, I heard a different kind of chant.

"Blue Lives Matter"
"Blue Lives Matter"
"Blue Lives Matter"

I thought it was strange that Blue Lives Mattered given the nature of the event, and so I turned to find the origin of the sound.

"Blue Lives Matter"
"Blue Lives Matter"
"Blue Lives Matter"

Earl smacked his teeth.

Earl: Hmm. See, Black folks can't have nothing.

I hated everything about that statement.

The chants grew louder.

"Blue Lives Matter"
"Blue Lives Matter"
"Blue Lives Matter"

Then Earl piped up, having seen something in the crowd.

Earl: Well would you look at that — the apple don't fall too far from the tree, now does it?

His laugh was that of a retired villain, raspy and exaggerated.

Roman: What apple?

Earl: You don't see your friend over there? That lil' supremacist-in-training?

I turned to where he was pointing. He was right. There was Jackson, holding a sign reading BLUE LIVES MATTER. He stood next to his father and held his sign high as his dad patted him on the back. A true father / son moment. Jackson gave his dad an awkward smile and they marched on.

I struggled to know what to even think of it. I was in awe, smacked in the face by someone I called my friend.

What now? If not my best friend, who could I trust?
Maybe Earl wasn't as crazy as I thought. Still… I wasn't
in the mood to hear his 'I told you so,' so all I said was…

Roman: Let's go.

The Metro was a little different than the "L" back home
in Chicago. I missed home, I missed my life as I knew it.
I'd been here about a year now, but it still wasn't home
yet. Home was where my parents were, and there I had
more friends, more family. It wasn't the worst being here
with Ma Ma and Pop Pop, it was just strange.

In sixty-five years I'd be Pop Pop's age. Time. I wondered
how much progress would be made. Progress.

I didn't love that word. I recognized the opportunity that
I had that my grandfather did not. I didn't know the
humiliation of a 'whites only sign' or having to be served
through the back door. I didn't know the stress and the
horror and the uneasiness of knowing that I could be
hung, spat on, kicked, that I was invisible.

But 'progress' to me still meant that there was no sense
of urgency to justice, that equality needed to take time,
that my grandfather had to wait, and his father too.
After Ma Ma handed me The Fire Next Time, *I started*
researching James Baldwin some more. I thought about

an interview I saw where he said, "What is it that you want me to reconcile myself to?" He said that he was always told that it takes time. He said that it had taken his father's time, his mother's time, his niece's time, his uncle's time. And then he said, "How much time do you want for your progress?"

Suddenly, back on the Metro, a man moved fast past me yelling, "Jesus saves!" He ran through the door and into the next train car. I hadn't thought about Jesus in a long time. I remembered when I first had my doubts. And I also remembered when I saw someone catch the Holy Ghost for the first time. I was a younger child so I was curious. They told me she was speaking in tongues and I remembered wanting to learn how, but I was told it was revealed from God.

God had yet to speak to me. I wondered why God hadn't revealed Himself to me or to anyone I knew.

What was faith?

And why would you ever teach a slave to have it?

And how could I — a descendant of those enslaved people — have faith?

We arrived at our stop, Tenleytown.

The walk home was nice. Pop Pop saw that I needed some space and so he allowed me some quiet. The weather brought us a sense of weightlessness.

Then, my phone dinged.

Jackson

Hey! What you up to? Cages
tomorrow?

*I looked at his message on my screen and released a long
sigh before shoving the phone deep into my front pocket,
reluctant to ever respond.*

*I got home and had to figure out what to do with myself
and decided I was due for a shower. When I got out I
found myself stuck again — what could I do? I didn't feel
like watching TV, so I went back outside to get some air.*

*When I stepped outside, Ma Ma was out on the porch
sitting in that chair that sways. I told her about the
protest and showed her the Instagram live that Pop Pop
was in. I asked why she didn't come and she told me that
it was us young folk's turn.*

*I sat with Ma Ma in silence a while before I finally let
her in on Jackson and his counter-protest.*

Carretta: Is Jackson your friend?

Roman: I guess, but after this I don't know. Should he be
my friend?

Carretta: I think you shouldn't decide until after you
speak to him and hear what he has to say.

Roman: I'm not tryna hear none of that.

Carretta: Watch your tone speaking to me. Now I know you're upset, but in life you can't avoid uncomfortable conversations. You just gotta face them head on.

> *I sat quietly, part of me taking in what she was saying, and the other half scared to speak. (Ma Ma is terrifying when you talk back to her.) I could see the sun starting to set. It was the moon's turn now. I decided to head to bed early. I walked up to my room, and before I turned off the light, I texted Jackson that I'd meet him at 3 p.m. the next day.*
>
> *It was time to see who Jackson really was.*

Sunday, May 31, 2020

(thwack)

I loved the sound the ball and the bat made when they connected.

Roman: So…

I stalled.

…what'd you do yesterday?

Jackson: Couple things with my dad.

Roman: Yea, I feel that.

(thwack)

He still wouldn't be upfront with me? I started to get even more frustrated. Jackson must have sensed the tension because he changed the subject.

Jackson: Would you rather be a shape or a color?

Roman: Color.

Jackson: Why color?

Roman: I feel like a shape is just an object. A color, though, has more possibilities… It's a bit more complicated, don'tcha think?

I waited for him to get my point.

Jackson: I don't know, but I think I'd be a sphere. But not small like a ball... I'd be a planet!

(tink)

I laughed. This man went for a bunt.

Roman: I thought you'd be a square.

(thwack)

Jackson: Why would I be a square?

He stepped away from the plate.

Roman: I saw you holding that sign.

(thwack)

Jackson stiffened. He looked away from me.

Jackson: Look, it wasn't my idea. I didn't tell you this, but the night before... my house got egged and spray-painted. Nasty stuff about cops. My dad made me join him and his cop friends at the counter-protest. I'm sorry...

Roman: Bullshit.

Jackson: What do you mean?

Roman: You held that sign like you wanted to.

Jackson: No, look. The job my dad does is a very dangerous job... I understood why...

Roman: You held the sign!

Jackson: You make it sound like I'm so terrible, like it was

MY knee that...

There was a pause. He caught himself, but that was all I needed to hear. I didn't think twice, I swung my bat at him. And even though he managed to catch it, the damage was done.

There was a stare down that seemed to last an eternity that communicated what words would not... that we might not speak again. I took one last look at who was once my friend and I walked off.

Later that day, Sunday, May 31, 2020

Point-of-view: JACKSON

*I kicked the little rock to occupy my walk home. I wasn't
a bad person. I wasn't a racist. I didn't do anything to
anybody, but somehow I was a racist? I tried so hard to
be a good person: I said please and thank you and excuse
me, I picked up trash off the streets, I followed the CDC's
guidelines and went out of my way to avoid old people
so I didn't get them sick. Roman was my best friend for
God's sake, the only Black kid in our class, and yet I was
guilty? Guilty of a crime I myself did not commit, but
just because I was privileged, white, and male.*

*I just felt scattered. Why were things so black and white
when there was so much gray area? It was very messy stuff,
too messy to think about. But I just didn't understand...
it was as if life was only hard for people of color. I knew
I was the majority here, and maybe that was the bedrock
of the issue, but there were so many efforts being made
for people of color, and then it was as if it wasn't enough.
When everything that could be done was being done.
When realistically thinking, it took time for change and
equality to happen. Well maybe it was that I just didn't
have it hard enough, but having a dad like I did, who
didn't hear or see me, it just didn't feel likely.*

I walked up to the front door, planning to avoid him,

but before I even got to put the key in, the door opened.
God dammit.

Mr. Anderson: You're back early.

Jackson: Hi, Dad… Yeah, I guess.

I grunted.

Mr. Anderson: You look upset.

Jackson: I'm fine.

Mr. Anderson: Your mother told me you were out with Roman.

Jackson: Yep

I tried to walk past him…

Mr. Anderson: Anything happen between you two?

Dad was always cool with Roman and I being friends, but I could still tell that he was always a little suspicious of him.

Jackson: No, we're good.

He knew I was lying.

Mr. Anderson: Alright let's go.

He took out the keys to his Jeep.

Jackson: Go? Go where?

Mr. Anderson: I don't know what happened between you

and your friend, but you two are going to hash it out...
with your words or with your hands, up to you.

Jackson: Dad! I'm really not in the mood. I just want to
sit on the couch...

Mr. Anderson: Fine, I'll make it simple: do you want to
hash things out with Roman or do you want to fight *me*?

I stood still and silent.

Jackson: Fine, then I'll fight you.

I said this before I could stop myself, and quickly recoiled.

Mr. Anderson: What did you just say to me, boy?

Welp, there was no turning back now...

Jackson: Why did you even make me go to that protest,
Dad?

Mr. Anderson: Make you? I can't make you do anything!

Could you believe this guy?

Jackson: What!? You woke me up, put me in the car, and
didn't tell me where we were going. You didn't give me
a choice, you just gave me a sign that said BLUE LIVES
MATTER and told me to 'make you proud.' And have you
ever tried saying 'no' to you? That's why I still let you think
I'm going to follow in your footsteps and become a cop!

Mr. Anderson: You mean Police Officer, young man. And
you mean the footsteps of my father's father, my father,

and me. What — you're too good to become a "cop"? You think you're better than us?

Jackson: Yeah, well, I'd also be following in the footsteps of Officer Chauvin, Officer Thao, Officer Kueng, and Officer Lane…

Mr. Anderson: Being an officer is a dangerous job, son! Now, that man did not deserve to die, but respectable police officers don't deserve to be ridiculed and shamed either…

Jackson: That's not the point, Dad! You don't respect me enough to allow me to make my own decisions and think for myself. And if I could choose to think for myself, I wouldn't have gone to that counter-protest with you. I mean a man was murdered by police officers and you want to show up and undermine his death like his life didn't matter. And I can't believe that I was there holding signs with you!

And I couldn't believe that I defended me being there to Roman…

Mr. Anderson: These things are complicated. *Everybody's* life matters, and these BLM thugs are pushing people to hate people like ME who are here to protect and serve.

I shook my head and walked into the house.

129

Trump mobilizes military, threatens to use troops to quell protests across U.S.

June 1, 2020

Police officers wearing riot gear face off against demonstrators outside of the White House.

Koshu Kunii

President Trump holds a Bible as he visits St. John's Church near the White House on Monday.

Shealah Craighead / The White House

President Trump militarized the federal response to protests of racial inequality that have erupted in cities across America late Monday, as authorities fired tear gas at people protesting peacefully near the White House to disperse crowds moments before Trump staged a photo opportunity there.

Wednesday, June 3, 2020

Point-of-view: ROMAN

I spent the next couple of days watching the world's outrage on social media and thinking about why our president tear-gassed peaceful protesters outside of the church for his little "photo opp." It seemed like racial tensions were so high they even caused a rift between me and a friend I loved like a brother. Which sucked. And on top of everything else, I'd had to find somewhere new to swing. With all this on my mind, sleep didn't come easy.

I finally heard the noise that the chairlift makes when he goes up or down stairs. It was still dark outside and the birds were still whistling. I decided to join Pop Pop on his morning roll. I bounded down the stairs.

Earl: Aww hell.

I looked at him.

Earl: You can't be doing that, grandson, I almost reached for my ankle.

I laughed. A Panther never retires...

Roman: I thought I'd join you today.

Earl: That's fine, just announce yourself next time.

The first forty seconds were silent. I wanted to ask him about Sherman but I asked around it instead.

Roman: What was war like?

Earl: Hell. War is hell.

Roman: Did war change you?

Earl: Boy, why you asking me all these silly questions?

I decided to go for it.

Roman: How did you and Sherman actually meet?

His face didn't enjoy the question.

Earl: Basic training.

Roman: Well did you guys share a bunk? Receive the same punishment or something?

He just looked at me.

Roman: Maybe you guys were grouped together for some type of exercise?

I thought these were very valid questions. I mean how did they become friends?

Earl: Does this have something to do with Jackson?

Ma Ma must've told him about our fight.

Roman: I guess so…

I let it sit for a moment.

Roman: You said you and Odecky were friends too, right?

Earl: We were. War is hell. You need someone to go

through it with. And Odecky would stick his neck out for me when some of those Southern boys got out of line. You need someone to confide in when things get tough emotionally. We talked about family, showed each other the pictures of our gals, talked about what we'd do when we'd get home… That som bitch saved my life in a way too. He was just as important as the rifle in my hand.

It took a moment for me to realize that he had finished speaking. I didn't know what to do from there so I became okay with the silence.

It was nice; I watched the sun yawn and saw the day as it crept into fruition. Around us, the neighborhood was starting to come to life, with lights coming on and the sounds of kids' voices coming through windows.

Pop Pop suddenly felt vocal again.

Earl: …and so when we got home, I not only thought that Odecky and I would stay close, but even thought that maybe, if he and I were able to get over our racial differences, America could, too.

He cleared his throat.

Truth be told, years after Odecky passed me on the street, he wrote to me. I held his letter in my hand. But I never opened it. I threw that letter right in the trash. I didn't know if it was an apology or if he was dying. I didn't care. By that point, I had already seen where I stood… with him

AND with America.

As we neared the top of the hill, I solemnly watched a man who I'd never seen so vulnerable. I could see in his face that he was hurt. Tears gathered at the corners of his eyes. I knew that, at any moment, he could break down and cry. I realized that my grandfather wasn't just angry, he was in pain. He lost a friend.

A moment went by.

Earl: What if, for whatever reason, you and Jackson never speak again? Would you resent him?

Roman: Probably.

Pop Pop raised his fist and brought the full weight of his emotion down with it as he hit the armrest on his wheelchair.

Earl: Well… you'll resent the world, too.

Thursday, June 4, 2020

What is it to love, to befriend? What does it mean to argue and make amends?
What is it to resent, to scorn? What does it mean to be willing and forgiving?
What is pride, what is bitterness? And what does it mean to be better for overcoming it?

After seeing how Pop Pop was hurt by his broken friendship, I saw how disappointment could dismantle trust. I didn't want that for me. I mean, what happened with me and Jackson wasn't as big as what happened between Pop Pop and Sherman, but it could still have the same effect. True friends should be able to have difficult conversations and resolve conflict, right? I believed Jackson to be a true friend, a confidante. And I might not have a rifle, but if I did, I believed Jackson would be just as important.

I'd spent the last week feeling hurt and angry. And I needed that. But maybe now the more productive thing would be to hash things out — at least to try — so that I didn't end up resenting the world, too.

I tapped 'New Message' on my phone.

Roman

Cages?

Jackson

Be there in 50 mins.

Roman

Bet.

Later that day, Thursday, June 4, 2020

Walking up to the cages was like nearing a cliff overlooking a battlefield. I felt awkward, anxious, but prepared. The last time we spoke, it didn't end too well, but things should be fine... right? I walked up to our usual spot and waited.

Jackson's nerves walked in before he did. I saw the uneasiness in his face.

Jackson: Hey dude.

Roman: 'Sup man.

Jackson: I'm sor—

Roman: Here, take this.

I interrupted him and handed him a bat. He flinched.

Jackson: You're not gonna swing it at me again are you?

He smirked. I said nothing.

Jackson: So... I spoke to my dad.

Roman: How'd that go?

Jackson: I finally stood up to him.

Roman: What do you mean?

I knew Jackson's dad could be rough. I'd seen him curse Jackson out for jay-walking.

Jackson: Told him I didn't want to be a cop. And that we were wrong to be on that side of the protest.

Roman: "We" were wrong??

Jackson: *I* was wrong…

I nodded my head at Jackson, allowing myself a smile as I walked up to the plate. I let the moment carry itself and embraced things becoming normal again. I was happy — hopeful, even — that our friendship was stronger than whatever this country could throw our way…

Roman: …If you had a genie, what would you wish for?

Jackson: Megan Thee Stallion.

I laughed so hard that I had to take a step back to collect myself.

THWACK!

kai.g_ss

kai.g_ss This fence is representing that you cannot get to us. Basically, it's the guy in power saying, 'You can't get to me.' But now with the wall and the mural and everything, it's kind of like the Berlin Wall before they took it down, everybody had to put stuff on it to represent, like, we are here for a cause, we are here to fight for something that's dear to us, dear to everybody.

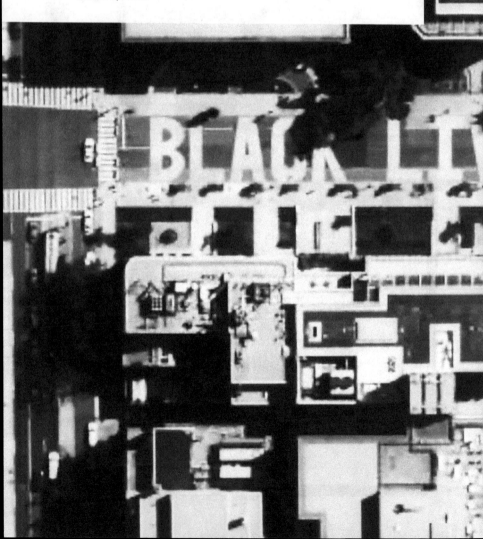

DC Paints Street, Designates It 'Black Lives Matter Plaza'

June 5, 2020

In Photos: Looking Back On 12 Days Of Protests In D.C.

June 11, 2020

Vlad Tchompalov

The District has seen 12-straight days of demonstrations following the police killing of George Floyd in Minneapolis, drawing tens of thousands of protesters to downtown and the surrounding suburbs.

The ongoing protests have been marked by striking images of a city in the grips of a pandemic: streets flooded with throngs of masked demonstrators; law enforcement agencies and military personnel descending on the city by the busload; and fencing, barricades and uniformed officers blocking the public space around Washington's landmarks.

The early days of protests saw clashes between protesters and law enforcement officials, who used tear gas, pepper spray capsules, rubber bullets and low-flying helicopters to disperse crowds. But the long days and nights of demonstrations largely have remained peaceful — and, at times, jubilant — as people from across the D.C. region have gathered to demand change and action on police and criminal justice reform.

Clay Banks

A LITTLE KING IS ON THE RISE

by Tatiana Robinson

Friday, June 12, 2020

There's a new urgency in the city. A new anger. With the murder of George Floyd a few weeks ago, it's like the city has gone crazy — not just the city, the whole country. Every day there are new flyers on Instagram about another protest. "I can't breathe!" It's the main thing I hear when I turn on my TV every morning, walking to work, you name it…

COVID is already a stressor by itself, but now we have to worry about losing our people. First, they took Breonna Taylor. Now, they got George Floyd. This one hit too close to home. I remember when they took my dad away from me — I was only 8 years old. As a Black man, I'll never feel safe, especially if my life is left up to police officers who get too power-hungry. Now I'm 22, and I live in Southeast

DC with my mama and my 6-year-old son. My everything. Every day I worry about him, and I can't bear to tell him the hard truth: This world wasn't built for us.

I don't want my son to grow up like I did. I mean, I never really got to know my father. He was so young when he got shot. Barely got to live his life. They said he "fit the description." But before they investigated, they killed him. He wasn't even the one who did it. My biggest fear is that history will repeat itself: that my life will be cut short, that my son will not know me. My young King is the most important thing to me in the world.

"No Justice, No Peace!" I hear them screaming blocks away while I'm at work.

I work at a local Black-owned clothing store downtown. I love working for Mr. James — he's easy to get along with since we come from the same place, and even though he's an old head, the knowledge he drops is crazy! Somehow he continues to find new creative ways to keep people interested in his clothing. I hope to have my own clothing line someday. "King's Wear" is what I'd name it, after my son. I can't wait to see my logo plastered on a storefront. And maybe my son can even become my business partner someday. One can dream...

"SAY HIS NAME!" I hear the protesters getting louder and louder.

"Hey, Mr. James, can I talk to you for a sec?" I ask, approaching him. "Do you hear these protesters? I'm wondering if we should close up. It might get dangerous out there."

"Yes, I hear them," Mr. James replies. He sets down the folded pile of hoodies in his hand. "I hear them and I support them. That's why we're staying right where we are. If we always let our fears take over, King, we'd get nowhere as a people." He looks at me and waits. He knows I'm coming back at him — it's what we do.

"Yeah, but at what cost?" I ask. "Those folks out there got families to go home to. What if they get arrested, or worse, killed?" I'm worried about the safety of these people. They just killed yet another Black man. How is protesting going to help?

"I get your fears, but if not now, then when? If we don't fight for what we believe in, then who will?" says Mr. James.

He goes deep in thought for a while, then says: "When I was young, they told me I'd be in jail by 15. I had to prove them wrong and speak up for myself. Do you think it was easy for me to open my own store? If I'd let the fears of not making it creep in, I would've got nowhere. I wouldn't have met you."

I wonder what I'd be doing if it wasn't for Mr. James. I love working at his store, plus he's a great family friend. And honestly, I don't know if I'd have been able to make it this far if I hadn't met someone like him.

"You have a point, man, but I have Lil' King to think about. It's too risky. I mean, look at my father, killed by a cop. George Floyd, killed by a cop. Thousands of other Black men, killed by a cop. And you want me to go shout in the face of a cop and say stop it? I can't put myself in that situation." Just thinking about it, my heart pounds. I mean, what if that puts a target on my back? I can't imagine losing my son for a protest.

Mr. James places his hand on my shoulder and looks me in the eye. "I know that because of what happened to your father, this will forever be a hard topic. But only you can control what you do, and how you use your voice—"

I interrupt. "Look, with all due respect, you don't get it."

Mr. James just nods his head. "I'll lock up. Head home to spend some time with Lil' King. I'll see you tomorrow."

I take a deep sigh. "Thanks, Mr. James. See ya."

As I walk to the Metro station, I'm thinking over what he said. I tell myself I'm staying out of it because I don't want to get hurt, and plus we're in a pandemic — the CDC says to stay away from large groups. But really, how can I just sit here quietly like nothing's happening? I care. I mean, what if that was me, or even worse, my boy. My young King. I can't even begin to imagine how I'd feel.

I take the train home. It's a quick ride — Gallery Place to Anacostia. When I get there, I unlock the front door to my apartment. Just like any other day, I am greeted by the screaming television playing Lil' King's cartoons. I look around to scan my home. Same as always. The pull-out couch that only has three sections (enough for our family), the black coffee table (the center of everything), and Lil' King's favorite, the TV. Toys are cluttering all over the floor. The only organized thing seems to be a tower that was being built on the black coffee table. The tower is made of colorful wooden blocks, and by the looks of it leaning, I'd say it was built by Lil' King.

I plop down on the couch and let out a loud groan. I close my eyes for not even half a second when a little person jumps on me. "Daddy!" screams Lil' King. "You're home." If I ever think anything is wrong, all I have to do is look at his smile, and it makes everything worth it.

"Where's Grandma?" I ask.

"She's lying down," he replies. "You know we get tired waiting for you to come back, Dad." I can tell by the tone of his voice that he is getting a little sad. "We were taking a nap, and I heard the door."

I never wanted Lil' King to feel like this. Like I don't make enough time for him. But it's hard, ya know? Balancing work and him so we can keep the bills paid. But I'm the man of the house, so I gotta work to keep the lights on. I just have to figure out a way to do both. Maybe I can find a way to spend time with him tomorrow.

I pull out my phone to text Mr. James.

King

> Hey, Mr. James. Can I make tomorrow a bring-your-kid-to-work day? I want Lil' King to see the store and spend some time with me.

As I wait for the text, Lil' King leaps onto my lap with the biggest smile ever. Staring into his eyes is like the weight of the world is off my shoulders.

Hopefully, Mr. James will let me bring Lil' King. It'd be great to spend the day with him. I know he'll be really excited. Plus, it'll show him that I'm trying… or at least I hope it will.

King squirms off my lap and runs to get something from his room. Sometimes I just can't tell with him. He's happy when I'm around, but what about when I'm gone? I know I'm not happy when we're apart. I don't know how to show him that I'm doing my best. But one day at a time, let's worry about that later…

My thoughts are interrupted by the vibrations of my phone. The notification tells me that I have a new text.

Mr. James

> Of course. Can't wait to see the little fella again. See you tomorrow morning

Mr. James is a lifesaver! This is a start, and we'll go from here. Lil' King will be so excited.

"Hey, King!" I yell out.

"Coming, Dad," Lil' King yells back. Tiny feet run over our apartment carpet. He jumps onto my lap again.

"You wanna go to work with me tomorrow?" I ask him.

Before he responds, his face lights up. His smile stretches from ear to ear. These are the moments I enjoy most, just genuinely making him happy.

"I can't wait for you to see the store," I say.

Saturday, June 13, 2020

It's the next morning. Lil' King and I are running a little behind. We take the train. Lil' King takes in the sounds, the flashing lights, everything. All with a big smile on his face.

The Metro station is about a block from the store. Lil' King and I walk fast. Out of nowhere, the chants grow louder.

"I CAN'T BREATHE!"

Protesters shout in unison. There's no chaos in action, only people linked in arms. There's Black, white, and brown people, everyone out here. I pick up Lil' King.

"Why are they screaming, Daddy?" Lil' King asks.

"We're late for work. Let's hurry," I say, walking faster.

I don't know how to respond when he asks questions like this. I've been careful to turn off the news and keep him from knowing about George Floyd. I want to shield and protect him from the world, but I can't do that forever.

When we get to the store, Mr. James has already opened up shop. "Good morning, Kings," he says with a big grin.

Lil' King chuckles so hard he practically falls over. "Good morning!" he calls back.

As we set up the store, Mr. James reveals he wants to hold an important sale today, in support of the protesters. He hands me a big sign to hang outside the store that reads: "BLACK LIVES MATTER... FREEDOM

FIGHTERS GET 50% OFF."

I don't know how to feel about the sale. I mean, I see that Mr. James wants to support the fight, but it could be dangerous drawing too much attention to the store, especially while Lil' King is here. Maybe I chose the wrong day to bring him.

We take the time to set up the mannequins for the day, then we flip our sign to "Open."

Within twenty minutes, customers flow into the store with smiles on their faces. They are wearing t-shirts that say "Black Lives Matter," "Say Her Name," "Stop Killing Us," and "Your Silence Will Not Protect You."

"Masks on please," I remind them as they enter. I pull out the box of masks for anyone who hasn't brought their own.

Despite the chaos outside, it's peaceful in here. Lil' King sits on the countertop interacting with customers, making them laugh. He throws a red-colored shirt back and forth with a man sporting long black locs with hints of blonde at the tips. Though I can't see their smiles, their masks move up and down as they laugh, and the joy in their eyes tells it all.

Just then, three protesters — it looks as if they're a family — rush into the shop.

The child looks as if he's about 12 years old. He holds a sign that reads "Black Kings Matter!" He follows behind his parents with a worried look on his face. The man helps the woman to walk as she leans on him.

"Hi, do you have any water? It's pretty hot outside,

and my wife is getting overheated," he says as he sits his wife in a chair near the front door.

"Is she alright?" I ask. She looks like she'll pass out, and I'm pretty nervous.

Just then, Lil' King runs over with a bottle of water. "Here, Daddy," he says as he passes it to me. He hides behind my leg, looking on with concern.

I hand the woman the bottle of water. We watch to make sure everything is alright. Her husband and son stay close to make sure she's alright, too.

While her husband fans her with a rolled-up flier, the boy approaches Lil' King and bends down to his level. "What's up, lil' man," he says as he reaches out to dap Lil' King up. Lil' King goes for a fist bump instead. I guess he remembers my reminder about germs during COVID.

Lil' King responds, "What's up." He adjusts his mask to ensure it's over his nose. Since his face is small, Lil' King's mask is always slipping down.

The two continue to talk as I help to ensure the woman is alright. I know Lil' King is feeling proud that a big kid is talking to him, so I try to act like I'm not listening. I overhear that the boy's name is Khalil. The man and woman are his parents. Then they're talking about Khalil's sign. He tries to explain to Lil' King what protesting is.

"A protest is when a lot of people come together to make their voices heard," Khalil explains to Lil' King. He tries his best to break it down to a 6-year-old.

My son, as always, is curious. "How do you do that? Make your voice heard?" Lil' King asks, looking at Khalil with his big, shiny brown eyes.

"You can write an idea down on a sign or shout out how you feel with the crowd!" Khalil explains. "When we share our beliefs and stand together, we can help make real change."

I get a little nervous. I don't know how much Lil' King should know about all this, especially since he isn't old enough yet, but he doesn't seem scared or anything. In fact, he seems eager.

"King, let's get back to work," I say. He responds with a smile, and the couple and their son head out.

"Thank you so much," the woman replies. "Remember you're a Black king," Khalil says to Lil' King as he gives him a fist bump.

Lil' King smiles as they head out of the shop.

We finish the busy work day, making sales all day to sweaty but energized protesters. We flip our sign to "Closed" as Mr. James pulls out the wood to board up the windows. It's been standard practice for all the stores downtown lately, though nothing has happened to our store besides someone spray-painting BLACK LIVES MATTER across our boards. I do know of some other stores that got their windows smashed nearby though. People are fed up and are ready to put up a fight.

Once we finish up with the hammering and whatnot, Mr. James explains that he's spending our usual Sunday off by going to a protest himself. "It's for our community — folks who actually live here on the Southside. It'll be around Southwest near my house off of M Street — to show our solidarity for George Floyd's family," he explains. He's been part of the planning committee and wants both Lil' King and me to attend. Though I'm hesitant, he affirms to me that it'll be kid-friendly, and they'll even have t-shirts for marchers to wear. And, after seeing how excited Lil' King got speaking to the protesters today, maybe it would be a good experience after all?

"It's tomorrow at 9 am. See you there," he says. We head out of the store. He walks in the opposite direction. I pick up Lil' King, and together we head for the Metro station. "Let's go home, lil' man," I say. It'll be a big day tomorrow, and we have a lot to prepare for.

Sunday, June 14, 2020

I approach Mr. James' house, holding Lil' King's hand tight. I can't really tell if I'm nervous, but I trust Mr. James, so I guess it'll be alright.

I knock on Mr. James' door. A few seconds later, he opens the door with a huge smile on his face.

"Kings, how are you feeling today?" he asks, motioning forward as we enter the house.

"Good, we ate a big breakfast and—"

"Waffles and bacon!" Lil' King screams. He rubs his belly and grins.

Mr. James laughs. "Let me grab my jacket, and we can head to the community center to get everything started. I've finalized everything, and you'll be handing out the informational flyers," he tells me.

I nod, unsure of what to expect. I look at Lil' King, who flashes his famous smile. It's as if he can tell that I'm nervous because I swear it all goes away when I look at that goofy grin.

We head out to the community center. On our walk there, the sun is shining so bright. Sweat begins to form on my forehead. As we make our way, so many people greet Mr. James. Young, old, everyone. It's pretty cool. It seems like he's so well-respected here.

Once we reach the Greenleaf Center on N Street, I'm less nervous than I thought it'd be. The center is a two-story beige brick building with big glass windows and one

main door with a ramp that leads to it. A simple place to
gather. I hope it has air-conditioning, so I can at least get a
boost of cool air. Big sweat stains have already formed on
my black shirt. It seems like it'll be a long, hot day.

A group begins to gather. I hand out papers, as
instructed. People approach with signs in their hands and
smiles on their faces. Mr. James begins to speak into the
megaphone. "We are here to speak out for justice. We are
small but mighty," he preaches, looking into the crowd.

People begin chanting together in unison. They shout,
"No justice! No peace! No racist police!" I haven't been
part of a protest crowd like this, only watching it from the
outside, and being inside feels different. It's like everyone is
one big family.

Despite the heat, there are families here participating,
too. Even children, some younger than Lil' King. "Come
on, Daddy, let's go!" Lil' King says as he tugs at my arm.
He begins chanting the same thing as the protesters. I
follow suit, holding his hand tight.

As we march, Lil' King throws his hands in the air
and continues to shout. He's in full protest mode, like he
knows what to fight for. I think I'm proud, but I don't
know if I should be. I'm also worried that passion will put
him in danger. I can't help it. It's hard to choose which one
is more important — justice, or safety. I want them both,
especially for my son.

Lil' King lets go of my hand and marches in front of
me. I look over at Mr. James and flash a smile. "Look at

him," I say to Mr. James. "He's like a pro." The woman next to me comments on how mature he seems, and I start talking to her about her own sons, not much older than mine. It turns out this lady knows my mother — they went to grade school together. DC can be such a small place sometimes. I look forward and continue to march.

All of a sudden, I realize Lil' King isn't there in front of me anymore. "LIL' KING? LIL' KING!" I scream, but I am drowned out by the other chants. I begin to panic. This is the worst thing that could have happened today, and it did. I look over at Mr. James, and he's shouting along with everyone else.

"Where's Lil' King?" I ask as I tap Mr. James on his shoulder.

"I don't know, but he can't be far," Mr. James replies. He must see the fear in my eyes because he says, "Hey now, I'll help you find him."

We split up and begin looking for Lil' King. I look everywhere, running up and down the sides of the crowd. We pass the Southwest Library and the Waterfront Metro station. Police cars block off the intersections and some of them are standing beside their cars, with riot gear ready just in case. I pause to take a short breath. My chest is hurting. I'm panicking. I don't know what to do. I can't lose my son. We should've never come to this protest in the first place.

The lights and sirens seem to never stop. There's so much noise! The reds and blues of a police car feel too much like fire, and there's not enough water to calm it down. And all of a sudden, I am 8 years old again, wanting my own father, yelling, and not knowing how to help.

As I'm lost in thought, a policeman taps me on my shoulders. My body tenses. I immediately throw my hands up and yell, "PLEASE DON'T SHOOT."

He steps towards me telling me to relax. "You looked frantic, so I just wanted to help. Is everything alright?" he asks.

"Yeah, I'm fine," I respond, walking away in the opposite direction.

I get myself together. I don't have time for all these feelings right now — I've got to find Lil' King.

I get up to the front of the group, where the younger people are gathered. There's a young boy who I think I've seen before — is it that kid from the store?

And then I spot him — there's my King, standing beside Khalil, holding up a sign reading "PROTECT ME. I'LL BE A BLACK MAN LIKE MY DAD ONE DAY."

I rush to Lil' King and pull him to the side. I know I can't be too hard on him, but he really scared me. I get on one knee and hold his little face in my hands. By the looks of him, he can't tell if I'm angry or not.

"Never run off like that again," I say to Lil' King. I hug him tight, too tight probably, but I can't help it. Tears fill my eyes. I don't know what I would've done if I'd lost him. He's my everything.

"I'm sorry, Daddy, I was just with Khalil and the other

kids," he replies, hugging me back. "I just wanted to march with them…"

He goes on to say that Khalil was about to try to help Lil' King look for me. I glance over at Khalil and he's watching us. When he sees me looking, he flashes a big grin and a thumbs up. It does make me feel a bit better — I know from experience how my people, no matter how young or how old, continue to look after one another.

"It's alright, I was just worried," I say. I can't tell him about the depths of that worry, where it all comes from. Not yet. Someday he may have to start shouldering that same fear, but… not today.

Just then, I feel a hand on my shoulder. "I guess you found him," Mr. James says. He leaves his hand on my shoulder for a long while. It starts to slow my pounding heart. Maybe he does understand, better than I think.

Lil' King tugs on my arm. I bend down to check on him, but everything seems fine. In fact, he's smiling.

"When are we going to the next protest?" Lil' King asks me, his face full of everything I'd want my son's to be — excitement, curiosity, and fearlessness. I reach out, and all I can do is hug him, my young King.

DC voices   protest quotes   protest murals   BLM

"

I have a young nephew who I'm literally seeing when I see a Black man get killed. Who I am seeing when they incarcerate the wrong people. Who I am seeing when I see police harass others. I feel it's my responsibility to stand up for him. We are not just fighting for George Floyd. It's every other unnamed Black man who is killed daily. It's every other Black woman [who] is killed in her house.

"

— Nay, of Arlington,
who declined to give her last name, on June 3 near
the intersection of Connecticut Avenue and H Street NW

"There's nowhere else for me to be. There's nothing else for me to do. Nothing else matters but fighting for people who have been oppressed long enough, never deserved it. And everything this country does have to be proud of, they owe to Black people, they owe to the people that they subjected the most. And beyond wanting to highlight and support that cause, it's therapeutic for me to be here, you know, to be here in solidarity with my people. This is the only way I can heal myself."

— Rasa, who declined to give their last name, speaking
at the LGBTQ rally in Columbia Heights on Sunday, June 7

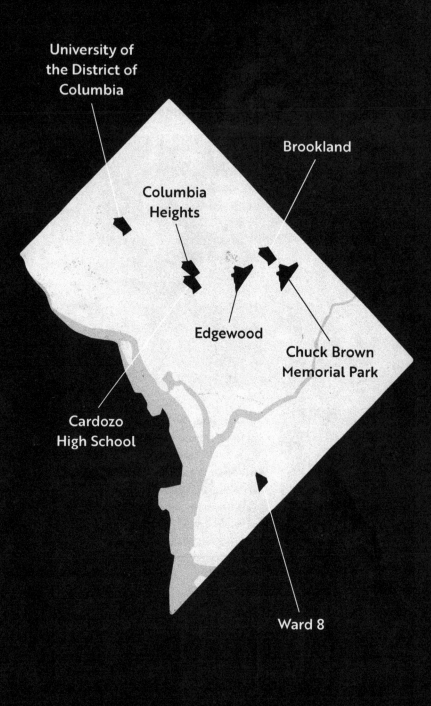

University of
the District of
Columbia

Brookland

Columbia
Heights

Edgewood

Chuck Brown
Memorial Park

Cardozo
High School

Ward 8

FALL

DAMAGED

by Saylenis Palmore

Abuelo

Living in a broken family is hard. It must be way harder than being president. To be honest, I never wanted to work harder than the president, so I never did. In my short-yet-long 18 years of life, I have tried to care about as little as possible... family problems included. It's too much stress and I'm too young for that. I don't like hearing my mom nag me about grades or listening to my brother complain or wondering where my dad could be. Instead I focus on making my own rules and spending time with my friends, so during my waking hours I'm usually as far away as possible from my family.

Well, that's not completely true. I always loved spending time with Abuelo.

My grandpa was born in Cuba and he immigrated to the U.S. just after my mom was born. Somehow he ended up in DC and just never left. Every morning he would drink his coffee, black, at the table, while I drank mine with a splash of milk, dipping in crackers and cookies as he described his childhood adventures. Some telenovela was usually playing in the background, and he kept at least one window open year-round. He said the fresh air was good for the soul.

Man, he had the best stories. I remember one day he told me about when he would go down to the Soroa River with his brothers and sisters back in Cuba. They would swim for hours and eat mangoes that fell from the trees. There was a rope tied to a tree and he and his brothers would swing as high as they could to jump into the water below. One time he flung his body on the rope and the branch snapped as soon as he swung over the river. He said he had bruises for a week.

There was another time that he and one of his brothers snuck into town one morning, about thirty minutes from his house, to buy candy from the stores. They only had some scraps of metal in their pockets, so the store owner felt bad and gave them one piece each for free. Abuelo laughed every time he told one of these stories, his voice a little raspy from the cigars, but still deep, saying, "But that was a long time ago."

My mom would stand in the kitchen shaking her head as my eyes grew wider and wider with each new tale. She would tell me that his stories weren't true, that it was just his imagination and that I shouldn't get any ideas. She'd say to him, "You know, you never told me that story before…"

True or not, I didn't care. I figured Mom was just jealous because when she was my age Abuelo was out working all the time. But since he retired, this was our morning routine: drinking coffee, sharing stories, and my mom telling us we both live with our heads in the clouds. Abuelo was the father figure my real dad could never be.

And so, the day I lost Abuelo? That day my life broke into 'Before' and 'After.'

Before
Saturday, September 5, 2020

Here's who I was in the Before:

Snoop Dogg and Wiz Khalifa's "Young, Wild and Free" blasted through the speakers. Bruno Mars' singing felt like it was piercing my body as Udoye sped through the tunnel. He was going at least 80 miles per hour, but I could see every line on the road coming to us in slow motion. My hand was catching balls of air that hit my face and all I could do was laugh. My hair slapped my ears to remind me I was alive. I closed my eyes and I was on the most beautiful beach in the world with sea turtles dancing around me. I opened my eyes and DC's city lights blinded me. I closed my eyes again and I was flying over the ocean.

I just felt so free on nights like this. And most nights were like this. Almost every night, having a new adventure with my best friend, Udoye, finding a new corner of DC to party in. It was the end of summer — after the intensity of all the protests, just before the start of college — and I needed a RELEASE. Every morning I woke up feeling like I only slept two hours, but who cares? Besides my mother. I could not escape the annoying buzzing of her multiple missed calls. Most times, she would just call to say I needed to be more responsible and that I needed to start acting like an adult. But, if I was already an adult, why didn't she just treat me like one and leave me alone?

I mean was I really doing anything wrong? I'd been

locked in the house for like six months, my prom was canceled, and I graduated through a computer screen. I think I deserved a little fun. Anyways, I was going to go to college, wasn't I, and it's not like I ever asked her for money. I swear she never gave my older brother this much of a hard time. He even went to Philly for a week without saying anything to anybody and all she said was, "Just like his father — disappearing when he wants to." Rather than hearing her talk shit, I just got in the habit of ignoring her calls and living my life instead.

The Last Morning with Abuelo
Sunday, September 20, 2020

One day a few weeks into the semester I woke up at
Udoye's house at noon. The night before had been a blast.
I'd been out pretty much the whole week, actually. I'd
made it to a few classes thus far — or at least part of a
few classes — but this online school thing was a joke. I
thought it might be better in college, but no. It was worse.
I mean, it was hard enough sitting in a classroom listening
to a lecture. But on a little Zoom screen? Whatever. Most
of it was recorded anyway. I could get caught up later.

The light was bright outside of Udoye's window, and
I could feel the warmth of the still-hot September sun.
Udoye was just starting to open his eyes.

"Udoye, are you excited?" I asked. He was leaving for
the Army soon. I couldn't imagine being without him.

"I mean, I guess," he said. "I'm definitely happy to
get out of here and travel… 'n hopefully not be broke
anymore."

We both laughed.

"I'm gonna miss you though," I said softly.

"You'll be good — you've got school." He paused. "You
actually gonna start going to class?" He was smiling but I
could tell he was also tryna be real.

I just shrugged my shoulders.

"What do you mean you don't know?" His voice got a
little louder.

I stayed quiet.

"Look at Alejandro. He didn't graduate because of whatever reason and now we only see him when he's working at Wendy's."

I was still quiet.

"Nobody knows what Eduardo is doing. He only hits us up for parties."

I still said nothing.

"And what about Michelle? She keeps saying she's going to finish school, but she can only take one class at a time because it's too expensive for her." He paused again, and again I said nothing. "You got a scholarship, Hermione! Don't throw it away. I'm not gonna be here for much longer, and then what will you do?"

"I know. I know. I know all of this. Damn." I finally spoke.

"All I'm saying is, we can do something with our lives. I'm going to the Army, you got school. Don't waste your time. Your mom and grandpa are counting on you. I mean, you're not named after the most driven character in Harry Potter for nothing!"

With the mention of my grandpa, I remembered it was Sunday morning.

"Fuck, I'm late!" I yelled as I hopped off the bed.

"Damn, don't yell like that! What are you late for?" asked Udoye, rubbing his ear.

"I told my grandpa I would stop by to see him today." I pulled open a drawer, looking for one of Udoye's clean shirts to change into. "You know, I go every Sunday."

"I'm sure he'll forgive you," said Udoye, rolling over. "I'm going back to sleep then."

"Ha!" I said, spotting my favorite Prince t-shirt. I threw it on and within minutes, I was already on my way to the bus stop.

After a thirty minute bus ride on the H2, from Van Ness all the way through Cleveland Park and Columbia Heights, I was finally outside my mom's house in Brookland. I could already hear my grandpa talking about something through the open window. I still had my key, so I just walked right in, ignoring how late I was.

"Abuelo! Good morning, how are you doing? Did you drink your coffee already? Did you save me some?" I shot question after question as I paraded through my mom's living room all the way over to Abuelo's seat. I gave him a big hug.

"Morning? Coffee? If I would have waited for you, the coffee would have been cold by now. It's almost 1 p.m., Hermione," he said, pointing to the clock on the wall.

I gave him a kiss on the cheek. "Ay, Abuelo, don't be so dramatic," I said.

"Where have you been anyways?" asked my mom.

"Oh, you know, around..." my voice trailed. "I went

to a party last night with Udoye. He's leaving soon for the Army, so we needed to celebrate."

"The Army? Oh wow." Mom sounded impressed.

Abuelo coughed. "And what about you?"

"What about me?" I said. "I'm good. I'm in school."

"And how's that going? We haven't heard much about it." He coughed again.

"It's fine," I lied. "It's whatever."

"It's whatever," said my mom. "Is that going to get you a good job?"

"You know, having fun is part of life, but you also have to think about what's next. You've got such opportunity!" said Abuelo.

"Oh my god! Everyone keeps talking about the future. Why can't we just live our lives, enjoy the moment? You know what I'm saying?"

"Hermione, your grandfather has a point," said my mom. "Every time I see you, you're talking about some party you just came from… and that's when I see you. Only God knows what you're up to when I don't see you for a whole week!"

"Look, all we're saying is start thinking about it," said Abuelo.

It was quiet. My eyes were now avoiding both of them at all costs. The carpet on the floor had never been so interesting to me. I was trying to concentrate on something else, but I felt myself getting upset. I was feeling warm and my legs were shaking a bit.

"And who says I'm not?" I yelled. "You guys don't know everything I have to think about." I grabbed my bag again. "I came here to have a good time with you guys and you're just judging me and telling me what to do."

"Ay, Hermione. Don't exaggerate," said my mom, as she walked back to the kitchen.

"No, I'm not exaggerating. It's true."

I kissed Abuelo on the cheek and could hear him saying my name as I walked out the door.

That night I went to another party with Eduardo, Michelle, Alejandro, and some other people from high school. Udoye was leaving the next day, so he didn't go. I couldn't stay at his place that night, but I didn't want to go home either. Instead, I went to Michelle's house. By the time we got to her place, I had lost count of how many times my mom had called and texted, but I honestly didn't care.

Like I said, that was the Before. Now here comes the After.

After

Sunday, October 11, 2020

It was three Sundays later that I lost him. October 11th, if you want to know the date. I won't ever forget it.

I'd been avoiding our usual morning routine since the last time. I just didn't want to be nagged again about my future. So I was at my friend's house making breakfast when I remembered my phone was dead. Within seconds of plugging it in, it started vibrating like wild. My cracked screen showed endless *Missed Call, Missed Call, Missed Call.*

About ten of the calls were from my mom. The others from some cousins. Not one voicemail or text, so I just kept stirring my eggs, minding my own business. *It couldn't be that important if they didn't even text or leave a message.* And then my phone rang. Mom. I picked up casually, already annoyed, but quickly knew something was wrong. She was talking really fast and she was crying. Her voice was shaking.

It was hard to understand her. "Your abuelo!" I heard. "Es tú abuelo… He's gone."

I still don't know if I actually screamed in that moment, or if my mouth hung open, silent.

I don't remember what I said back to her.

I don't remember hanging up the phone.

I don't even know how I made it onto the bus. Tears soaked my face as I walked down the aisle and collapsed in an empty row. I tried to picture one of his stories like I used to. I imagined the beach and the water, but nothing was in focus. I thought about the mangoes, but I couldn't imagine how they tasted. All I could see was the seat in front of me as I thought about how I should have gone to see him. I was on my way to MedStar hospital, hoping I could at least see his body, hold his hand. Hoping somehow if I got there in time it could all be undone. It didn't make sense, I know, but nothing made sense to me anymore.

Abuelo had been in the hospital for the past few days. They said he had COVID. Mom took him in because she was worried about his cough, and he'd tested positive. She told me the doctors were just keeping him there out of caution, because he was old. It seems foolish now, but at the time I was only low-key worried about it. I mean, he was so strong. I knew lots of people who had gotten COVID and it had been no big deal, they all recovered. And Mom said he was doing better. Since the hospitals weren't letting anybody in — maybe one family member a day — I never went to see him. I figured I'd wait until he was home, recovering. But now that he was gone, that seemed like a decision made in a dream, impossible to explain. I know my grandpa was old, but no matter how many times Death tells you he's coming, I don't think you're ever really ready to say goodbye.

I got to the hospital and a security guard stopped me just outside the automatic doors.

"Excuse me, can I help you?" he asked. He was stern,

unmoved.

"Uh, yes, I'm here to see my grandfather. My mother's in there with him. I don't know what—" I started to say when he cut me off.

"I'm sorry, Miss, but there's only one visitor per patient."

"But no! He's in there! They say he died!"

His face softened, but barely. "I'm sorry for your loss. But I'm afraid I cannot let you in."

I felt my body getting heavy, dropping to the floor as I closed my eyes. I couldn't see anything but the black back of my eyelids. My cheeks were soaked as I sobbed on the sidewalk. Someone said, "Get her some water! Get her some tissues! Miss, is there anyone we can call?" But I couldn't even lift my head to respond.

My grandfather was more like my own father. A *real* father. He was always there for me, even when I was a mess, and I wasn't there for him. Would I ever get over that? I couldn't imagine a life without him. With Abuelo gone, what would happen to us? What would happen to me?

Help
Friday, October 16, 2020

For the next few days, everything was a blur.

I'm not exactly sure what I did during this time. I slept a lot. Never at home. I couldn't bear to be with my family — their grieving would just remind me that when Abuelo needed me most, I stayed away. My mom had been calling. I never answered. Udoye never texted or called since he went away to basic training — he didn't even know Abuelo was gone. My other friends didn't know either, and they only wanted to go to parties. I'd rather just go for walks by myself.

Like now. I was walking again when I got a text from my mom:

> **Mom**
>
> Mija, please, I've been trying and trying to reach you. I am so worried. Your grandfather's service is tomorrow at 2 p.m. I really hope you'll be there.

I just kept walking.

I was somewhere around Columbia Heights when I saw an old man sitting on a bench. His beard went down to his chest. It was gray and looked dry. His beanie covered his head and his eyes were fixed on his boots. People passed by his cardboard sign as if it wasn't even there.

Hungry and poor. Please help.

I remembered my grandfather telling me of a vagabundo who lived in his neighborhood back in Cuba. I don't remember his name, but Abuelo said he had a long gray beard. I guess just like this man, except he was always barefoot and very skinny. Abuelo said he'd known this man before he became unhoused, and he was the nicest man he ever met. Then the man's wife and children died — some terrible accident — so he became depressed and lost his job. It wasn't long before he was on the streets of Havana, surviving off of people's kindness.

Abuelo told me his mother would always serve him a plate for dinner and would pack him some fruit, if she had some. The man always asked God to bless her and her family.

Usually I never gave money to people on the street, but, today, Abuelo was on my mind, so I checked my pocket — $3 — and I walked over to the man.

"Here you go," I said, handing him the dollar bills.

He looked up and smiled at me, slowly reaching for the money. "God bless you, my dear," he said in a low, raspy voice. "Thank you, thank you, thank you, my dear. God bless you."

He kept thanking me and that's when I noticed a couple of tents not far from where he was sitting. There were so many of these tents now — families who were victims of the pandemic in ways beyond just losing loved ones, like me. They lost jobs. They lost houses. I tried not to stare but when you really saw it, it was hard to look away. There was a shopping cart full of old bags, partially covered by a faded blanket. There was a woman sitting on the floor — she was about my mom's age — and there was a little girl sleeping next to her. She couldn't have been more than six years old.

On the corner of the block, I saw a younger woman, standing with another sign. She turned and I saw her face. She had dark eyes and dark, overgrown bangs. I squinted to realize I recognized her from my high school. She was maybe one or two years older than me. I didn't know her well, but I remember her sitting outside of the school, surrounded by friends. She was always laughing and having a good time.

She reminded me of me.

A siren started crying just up the street and I decided I should go. But, as I kept walking, I couldn't stop thinking about these people on the street. That could have been my family. That could be me one day. To be honest, I was scared. I started to think about what Udoye, Abuelo, and my mom had been trying to tell me. I needed to think about my future.

Yeah, I was in college, but I was barely passing my classes. I was barely even attending. I hadn't applied to any internships, and I definitely didn't have a job. I hadn't even joined any clubs on campus. No wonder everyone — including Abuelo — had been on me. Like, what was I doing with my life?

I kept walking around the city until it got dark. Michelle texted me about some DJ that was in town. I didn't respond. I kept walking and ended up at Cardozo, where I'd gone to high school. The grand old building was perched on the top of a steep hill, overlooking the city. I sat down on a bench and looked out at the lights. The weather was amazing. It would have been a perfect night for a drive or a patio party, but all I could think about was that family I saw earlier — and about Abuelo.

Abuelo had been an immigrant. The house he grew up in didn't even have running water, and he didn't want that for me, or my brother, or my mom. He came here for better, and he gave us better, but I was doing nothing to thank him. Nothing to show him it was worth leaving his homeland to come here. In this country, I knew you could be the person you wanted to be, and coming from a broken family with no dad was not an excuse to not keep going. I was choosing to throw my life away, and I had no one to blame but myself.

I broke down. My palms covered my face and soon my hands and cheeks were wet with tears.

In that moment, I just wanted my abuelo back. I wanted to thank him for all that he had done, and for all of the love he had shown me. I wanted to hug him and apologize for not doing my best like I promised him so many years ago. I wanted to make up for the Sundays I was late and the mornings I was gone. I wanted him to see me do better, but it was too late for that. He was gone now, for good.

Buzz, buzz. I looked down at the new text on my phone:

Mom

Hija, are you OK?

He was gone, but my mother wasn't.

All my life, I'd focused on not having a father in my life, so I never saw my mom as a blessing. Sure, she annoyed me with her phone calls and nagging, but I guess that's what moms do, at least moms who really care. All my life, I'd had my mom beside me… and now she was still here.

I'm Here
Saturday, October 17, 2020

When I got home it was late, and no one was awake. The house was quiet and dark. I went straight to my room, closed the door, and fell into the deepest sleep.

I don't know how long I slept, but by the time I woke up, the house was bright, but still quiet. It was 1 p.m. I had one hour to get to my grandfather's service. I took the fastest shower of my life, found a black outfit that didn't include a mini skirt or a crop top, and rushed out the door. I even splurged on an Uber ride to make sure the bus wouldn't make me late.

At 1:55 p.m. I pulled up to the funeral home. My mom was sitting in the front row of chairs. There were only about ten people there and the staff. COVID. I slowly walked up the aisle, avoiding the white casket at the front of the room. I would pay my respects to my beloved Abuelo soon, but I couldn't face him alone. For now, I focused on my mom. Her head was down and her fingers were playing with a folded tissue.

"Ma," I whispered, putting my hand on her shoulder.

When she looked at me, her eyes were puffy and a little red. They instantly began to water again. "Hermione, you came," she said, smiling ever so slightly.

"Yeah, I'm here, Mom."

She got up and gave me the tightest hug I've ever let her give me. I hugged her back and simply started to cry.

We stood there that way for a long, long time. I breathed in her scent. Café. She must have brewed it this morning, rich and black, just the way he liked it. Maybe she'd have another cup later, with me.

Together, we held hands and walked to the front of the room.

RIP abuelo

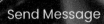

DEAR AL

by Darne'Sha Walker

Over It

It's Friday, October 23 — one year exactly since the worst day of my life.

While Bri and I are in our rooms, finishing up assignments for virtual school, everybody else is busy preparing for Al's memorial celebration. Grandma is outside getting the grill ready. I can't wait to help prep the burgers — that was Al's favorite. And I can hear Pat in the backyard, too, setting up tables and singing her heart out. The memorial celebration starts in just a few hours, and I still haven't written my letter yet. I've never been so busy on a Friday afternoon.

As soon as class is over, finally, I sign out of Zoom. I take out my notebook, connect my phone to my speaker, grab a pen, and try to start writing. I'm clicking the pen, trying to think of what I want to say. The letter is my way of expressing myself, even though I don't want to. I want to write something heartfelt that I can tie to a balloon and let go during the celebration — but when I try to put words on the page, it's just too much. Al knew I enjoyed writing and it was something he encouraged me to do. But how can I, now that he's gone?

Our cousins and some other relatives are the ones coming for the celebration. We all want to reminisce on the good times and get some good eats — you know, stay connected. I know they miss him as much as I do.

I write:

Dear Al,

And then proceed to tap my pen on the notebook. There's so much I want to tell him. Where to begin? I mean, he didn't even live to see the pandemic. He doesn't know about our new school, virtual learning, none of it. It's overwhelming enough to live through. How can I possibly put this past terrible year to words?

I get annoyed and rip the paper out of the book. I ball it up and throw it. *Why is this so hard? Why can't I talk to you? I wish you were here. All of this would be so much better.*

I take out my phone and immediately go to social media and start scrolling. It doesn't make anything better, honestly. I click on Bri's story and see pictures and videos of Al. I just can't watch them. Still. I swipe left and there's a girl from our new school on her story ranting about Amy Coney Barrett. Who? I tap and see a video collage of Breonna Taylor. Can't do it. I swipe again and it's a graphic about votes being thrown out. This stupid election hasn't even happened yet and people already trippin'. I exit the stories and see folks arguing over whether or not school should be open. Ugh. Keep scrolling. Then I see @DC_Problems posted pictures of six individuals who were shot and killed this week. And just like that, I was over it — this is enough social media for me. Most of it is BS. Most of all of this is BS. People have been dying — kids have been dying — constantly in our city. We're protesting about what's happening in other states, which is fine, and we're arguing about politicians who ignore everything we say, but when are we going to wake up and do it for our own in our own city?

I need a break. I go into the kitchen to get a snack. Grandma's finished her cooking but now Bri's in there making noodles. Bri and I are technically cousins, but she feels more like a sister. We're both sixteen and we attend the same school and have a bunch of the same friends. We live together in a house with my big sister Pat and my nephew DJ, our grandmother, and my aunt — Bri's mom. Thanks to COVID, *everything* is virtual — work, school, shopping, hanging out, whatever — which means we're all together, all the time. It's kind of a lot.

Pat comes in from out back and gets some leftover

chicken out of the fridge.

"How was school?" she asks us both.

"Well, we'd probably understand more if we weren't talking to our teacher through a computer screen, and his Wi-Fi actually worked… Then we'd probably be so much more successful," Bri says. She starts laughing but I know she's actually quite serious.

"I really don't understand what he is talking about in that class. I just make sure I show up with my camera on," I say.

Pat starts the microwave and shakes her head. "Well *that's* not concerning at all…"

"No, really, like nothing is the same," says Bri. "If anything, the world just made high school so much more difficult. I hate virtual learning. It's no help unless I'm already good in the subject. None of this will help me progress, you know? I'm a hands-on learner, and it took COVID to teach me that. My grades look *terrible* on that progress report card we just got. I mean, it's not like I was doing so great before virtual learning, but at least you saw my growth. This sucks."

Bri's clearly over it. She's so angry all of the time now, grumpy and snapping at people out of nowhere. I get it. It's not just that virtual school is a mess, (which it IS), but that ALL the things are more complicated than ever. Al's gone, and it was our own classmate who took him from us. We can't even go to our neighborhood school anymore — they say it's unsafe. After Al's death, our grandmother moved us to another school across the river. A private school. We didn't want to go there. No thank you. The school doesn't fit us. The teachers aren't the same — they're strict, just like their lessons. And we barely even got to know the other kids before *boom!* — the world shutdown.

"Yeah I get it," I tell Bri. "We actually were happy to go to class at our old school. And if we were still there, our online classes would be so much more fun. These teachers are boring."

Bri nods in agreement, but she looks drained. No more energy to vent. Me neither. It just feels like everything is going downhill. Since our cousin got killed, everything has changed. Aside from switching schools, some of our family moved, and the house got strict — we couldn't walk to the store or go out with friends. Grandma thought it would be a good idea to keep us sheltered, away from the world. It was the only way she could keep an eye on us. And that was BEFORE the pandemic. So then when the shutdown happened, it was like a cloud swooped in with loud thunder, hard rain, and scary lighting. My grandma and aunt already didn't trust anybody, and now nobody in the family sees the world the same anymore.

Pat is eating her chicken, just listening to us go on and on about school, but she knows it's deeper than that. Then she looks down at her phone and sees the time.

"SHOOT! I gotta go get DJ. Tell Grandma I'll be back to finish setting up the tables."

Pat grabs her keys and heads out the front door. Pat is

the only one of us who really goes out into the world since the pandemic. I know it's still hard for her to leave the house, but some days she has to go into work, and she has to drop DJ off at her mom's house. It's still hard for all of us, but especially her, because she worries so much about DJ. Lately there have been a lot of shootings in the city, and it's like it got worse since it hit home. She has to raise her son in this city and can't do anything but worry about his future and what it will look like. She doesn't feel safe in our neighborhood, and she knows the police can't protect us.

It's nerve wracking. We all have each other's locations. We look at them when we haven't heard from each other and haven't made it home yet. I know my sister is having a hard time, but she's the backbone of this family, so she tries to keep it together for us. I watch her take deep breaths before leaving the house. And when she goes to pick up DJ, I know she's anxious. I watch her location avatar drive in circles — I figure she's stalling just to avoid getting out of the car. And Grandma? I mean she has always prayed over us every night, even before our loss. So nothing has really changed but her praying harder now.

I look down at my phone and see how fast time has gone by. I only have two hours now. I need to start writing.

The Things I Miss

It's officially been a year now, and when I look back, I can't imagine how much we've been through. Thanksgiving was our first holiday without him. It was usually one of the most fun days, but it wasn't the same without his goofy spirit. Christmas was even worse. At the new year we tried to start moving on, to focus on healing, but just when I thought I was making some progress, the pandemic began. Shutdown. Everything started to hit harder. Being in isolation, it was like I had to think about him every day. Spring break came and we couldn't even go anywhere, like we do every year. It's like every month there's a new obstacle for us to jump over, and even if we do jump over, we still can't move, we're stuck.

I know Al would definitely try to make the best out of this craziness. He loved cracking jokes. Even when we thought it wasn't funny, it was funny to him. Like, I could imagine talking to him about the pandemic and virtual school and the whole ordeal of staying in the house, and him being happy he missed it, like, "Man, I dodged a bullet!" And then we'd fall off the bed laughing. It's dark, but it's true. He could find the funny in anything.

And one thing for sure: we wouldn't be bored or sad if he was here, cause he'd make sure he ate up everyone's snacks and plucked everyone's nerves. He sure wouldn't be down for staying in here and staring at us all day. And OH BABY! Don't let it be one of them weekends where we had to get our hair done — his tender-headed self couldn't stand it.

Al was definitely the clown of the cousins. But there was one thing we could clown him about that he hated — that stutter! We constantly got on his nerves about it. My uncle would always say, "Watch out, y'all are gonna get a stutter from making fun of him so much." The funny thing is, I do stutter sometimes now that he's gone. Whenever I get anxious. Every time I stutter I think of him, how he would probably be laughing at me.

There's so much I wish we could have done and finished. I remember the summer before he passed, we were talking about what we'd do after high school. He wanted to become a firefighter, and I wanted to work with kids. I didn't ever think I'd be doing it without him, but I know he'd definitely tell me to keep going.

At least these memories are making me smile. But when I try writing them down, nothing comes out. I want to tell him about how much we miss him, and how much I miss laughing with him. But every time I try to just say it, I get irritated. I don't really know why. But I always do. I put on some music and sink back into my bed, waiting for inspiration. Or courage. Or anything.

Ten minutes pass and I still haven't written anything. I can feel my pulse racing with the deadline approaching, even as I can't move. Grandma knocks on the door.

"Hey little girl, what are you doing?"

"Just writing," I lie. "Is everything okay?"

"Just checking to see what you was doing. When you finish, I need you to go downstairs and bring up some chairs for me."

"Okay, I'll be out in a second."

I pick up my phone and check out Find My Friends. I see that Pat still hasn't left DJ's grandma's house. I text her to see when she'll be back. My phone pings immediately. It's Pat saying they're on their way. I tend to get anxious when I know someone isn't where they usually are. I wonder if that will ever stop.

I look at the clock. One hour until the fam starts to arrive. How am I going to do this?

Too Close

When I leave my room, I see Bri on the couch in the living room and she is looking irritated. I say, "You good, Brodie?"

Bri responds, "I need to get out of the house. I'm losing it."

Grandma looks at me and says, "Why don't you take Bri to help you bring those chairs up out of the basement." Bri rolls her eyes and gets up off the couch to go with me.

I think I should talk to Bri while we're down there. I mean, I do understand why she's being so bratty. She's been having a hard time with this one-year anniversary, too. One whole year that he's been gone, and it's still unbelievable. His life was taken and there's nothing we can do about it. She's tired of being stuck in the house with memories of Al that won't leave her alone. She just wants to go out with friends to grab something to eat or even go skating, but she can't. Everything has become overwhelming, and especially today. So I do get why she's upset, but come on — we're dealing with enough as it is.

When we get down to the basement, I say, "I know you're frustrated and you're not having the best day, but just remember we're going through this together."

Bri responds, "I don't know what's going on, but I'm starting to feel a lot of different emotions and I can't deal with it. I just need to clear my head before everyone gets here. It's going to be a lot of tears and sad faces and I just feel like I'm not ready, you know? I just need to get out for a bit. I need a moment to breathe."

I look down and take a deep breath and say, "Yeah, I hear you." *I kind of feel the same way and Lord knows I'm tired of being in this house, but today is not the day.* "I know it's crazy and I'm sure we all would like to go somewhere, but today is the day we need each other the most. As much as people might be laughing and smiling, we all really feel the same way. So... we gotta thug it out, soldia."

Bri shakes her head and replies, "I'm over it. I need to go somewhere that's not here." She drops her chairs and goes back up stairs.

I stand there staring at her confused, "You're not gonna help me? BRI! The chairs?"

Bri just keeps walking up the stairs. I smack my teeth and try to grab all four chairs... struggling. My phone bings. At this point, I'm over it, too. I drop the chairs and grab my phone. It's Pat, texting that she's outside and needs help with DJ. I reply "OK" and head upstairs, leaving the chairs behind.

As I'm walking up the steps, I can hear Bri arguing with her mom because she wants to leave the house and her mom's telling her she can't.

"I'm tired of being in this house! I'ma do what the hell I want!"

My aunt smacks her in her mouth. It feels as if all the air got sucked out the room.

Bri looks shocked. Tears stream down her face before

she finally yells, "I'm leaving!" She pushes past me as she walks out the door.

I look at my aunt and shrug. Ain't nothing you can do to stop Bri when she gets like this — we've seen it before. But she'll calm down eventually. Hopefully in time for the memorial.

I follow her out the door to help Pat with DJ. She's just unstrapped him from his car seat and he's squirming, antsy to get out and run around. Pat hands me DJ and goes to get his diaper bag and stuff out of the trunk. Bri walks right past Pat without even looking at her.

"Where you going?" Pat asks.

Bri keeps walking. And then, just as soon as she gets to the end of the driveway, shots ring out.

Pop. Then again. *Pop, pop.*

And suddenly I'm running, running back to the house, shielding DJ with my arms. I can hear Bri and Pat running behind me. We all push through the door and dive onto the floor. The shots continue. I can hear Grandma in the kitchen speaking in tongues. I'm holding onto DJ as tight as I can, tears rolling down my face. So much fear. DJ's just looking around and he doesn't have a clue what's happening. Everyone is in shock.

We lay there until we hear sirens.

Then, finally, we get up and try to get ourselves together. I give DJ to Pat and all she can do is cry and kiss him. Bri can barely catch her breath, she's crying so hard. She starts apologizing to Auntie immediately.

"I'm sorry, Ma, I just wanted to go for a walk to clear my head. I miss my cousin and we've been stuck in this house for a year. I'm so sorry! I didn't mean—"

As Bri continues, I walk upstairs. All the feelings start hitting me at once and I can't be around all these other different emotions. I feel like a levee broke in my brain. Like I'm about to drown.

A Sign

By the time I get to my room, tears are running down my cheeks. I close my door and turn my speaker on as loud as possible and scream into my pillow.

I'm panicking. I try to control my breathing, but I can't. I don't know exactly what's going on, but it's not the first time. It happened at Al's funeral, too. All I can see is black. My mind goes back to that day and my body relives that terror, disbelief, anguish, all over again. I can't stop it. All I can do is cry and cry until finally my body is drained and I cry myself to sleep.

I wake up to somebody knocking at my door. It's Grandma coming to check on me. She turns down the speaker, sits on the edge of my bed, and puts her hand on my back. She tells me they postponed the memorial celebration to another day. It was just too triggering to still do it today. I can't even respond to her. I just think, *Thank God.* How could we possibly?

All I can do is think about what could have happened. One of us could have gotten shot — or worse. The thought of losing another loved one on the same day is mind-boggling. You never know what's gonna happen. It's still unbelievable that he's gone. But after today, it just goes to show that none of us can know if tomorrow is promised.

As I lay there, trying to fall back asleep, I hear his song playing on the speaker. "Ghetto Angels" by NoCap. But instead of making me sadder, his song soothes me. Makes me feel like he's here with me, in this room. I've been holding the pain all in for so long, and it's brought so much anger. But now it's like he's there telling me I have to get through this for us. I feel calm, and I get this quiet, powerful feeling like he's giving me strength. Like he's giving me a sign.

I look at the clock. Not yet midnight. I still have time.

So one year later — to the day — I think it would only be right to send Al something as my final goodnight.

Letting Go

After I finish the letter, I sit back and let the feeling wash over me. I did it. What was so hard for so long has finally been conquered. I want to believe that will be true, again and again.

It's quiet in the house. Everyone else is sleeping. I'm grateful for their rest. And I'm grateful for the chance to do this on my own, without anyone getting in the way.

I creep down the stairs and out the back door onto the porch. The balloons are still there, swaying in the cool night breeze. I untie one from the railing and go back into the house, up the stairs, past my room, into the attic. With the balloon in one hand and my letter in my teeth, I crawl out the window and sit down on the roof.

"Now I understand why you liked it up here so much," I say aloud. This was Al's favorite place, a secret escape that only the cousins knew about. As I look up at the sky and see the stars stretching out in all directions, I feel at peace. It is extremely quiet, which makes my thoughts very loud, but I understand the relief of being up here. I understand why his thoughts always changed after coming back down.

I still feel his presence with me, now even stronger. I clear my throat and begin reading him my letter.

Dear Al,

I miss you like crazy. Well, we miss you like crazy. A lot has changed. A lot of us disappeared, not knowing what to do after losing you. And it hurts so much to know that everyone in the family is hurting, but we're hiding it so we can 'be strong' for the others. Why do we do that? We're all feeling the same type of hurt. There's no need to hide it.

I understand now the importance of letting people know my emotions. I've learned that holding things in doesn't help, it just builds anger. And that anger can be taken out on the wrong person. I was so close to losing someone else today, over nothing. I can't let this happen to me. I won't.

I became distant after you died. I wasn't myself. Even living in the house with other people, I stayed in my room a lot. You used to give me these long talks and I used to be like "boy, I'm oldest"... Those speeches would definitely come in handy right now. Even with you being gone, the things you said then mean so much to me now. I see that in life — I don't realize how much I need something until it's gone. The people I love, I've learned to cherish them and make sure they know every minute of the day with no doubt that I love them.

I know if you were here, you'd tell me to straighten the f up, and I'm trying to, but it's gonna take a minute. I'm gonna get it, though. For you. For me. For us. It's crazy that I never really said these three words, but I think it's time, so here it is: Rest In Peace. I love you, forever.

~ Love, De'Asia

It feels good to hear my words out loud. And as soon as I finish, it's so quiet again. The trees blow gently in the wind and the leaves shake their soft reply.

I roll the note up and tie the string of the balloon around it, like a scroll. I take a deep breath and feel my eyes watering. As I begin telling Al that I love him, my hand gently lets go of the balloon. My stomach gets butterflies like I wasn't ready, but it's like I can feel him standing over my shoulder letting me know, *it's time.* Together we watch the balloon drift up, up, up. It flies higher than I expected, like it's touching the moon. And when the wind rustles the trees again, what I hear is: *I love you, too.*

DEMOCRACY HOW?

by Joseph Chuku

Prelude: Leaving Nigeria

It was December of 2017 and the Nigerian airport was hectic. People drowning in their own luggage. Merchants and patrons in a hurry to go about their business. A lot of transactions. A lot of noise and distractions. Telephones ringing. People rushing to make their flights, pushing against and through the small Edu family.

With a firm hand on Dennis' little shoulder, his father looked in his eyes with an intensity. "You are the man of the house now, and a man is supposed to provide. Work hard. Pursue your dreams. Take care of your mother."

These were the last words Dennis' father spoke to him before he boarded the plane to the United States. *How?* Dennis thought. He was only 14 and, whenever he had a problem, his parents solved it for him. Now, he was leaving his father in Nigeria with the task of taking care of his mom. And who knew what kind of problems they would find in the United States…

Tuesday, October 27, 2020
Almost three years later

Dennis sits on his front porch looking over 5th avenue NE. Though the street is normally busy and full of life — kids playing and dogs barking at each other — it is now dull, with few people on the street, their faces grim.

He still remembers the seriousness on his father's face, the last time he saw him. Almost three years later, and America is as foreign as ever. Lately, DC has felt even less like a place to call home. The marches downtown truly opened his eyes to the risk his dark skin poses. Not to mention, the exclusion he now feels being both Black AND an immigrant. And now, in the nation's capital, one week before the upcoming election, Dennis feels the pressure. The right outcome is critical in helping him reach his dreams of supporting his family... of making his father proud.

Dennis' citizenship status has been on hold ever since Trump was elected president. Lately, he's been spending his mornings before virtual school on his porch, wondering what the election might mean for him. This morning is no different. His legs start shaking. His mother comes out in a hurry, leaving for work, and sees her son in his new-formed routine. She's in her dark blue nurse's uniform, and holds a bag full of antiseptics.

Though Dennis tries to hide his anxiety from his mother, she notices everything. She takes a long look at her son, gives him a warm hug, and says tenderly, "Don't

overthink it. Let yourself feel it," before putting on her
mask and running to the bus stop.

That's not realistic, Dennis thinks while shaking his
head. He looks down at his phone to see another news
notification with the title "Why You Should Vote." I wish
I could, Dennis thinks, feeling helpless. He notices the
time. 8:00 a.m.

He runs to his room. Clears the dirty clothes on top
of his work desk. Looks around the floor, past sprawled
shoes, snack wrappers, and old notes to find his laptop
and charger. The time is now 8:20 a.m. as he finally sits
down to join his class. "You're 5 minutes late, Mr. Edu.
It's becoming a habit." Mr. Proctor says, sternly. Dennis
doesn't respond. "What is the excuse this time?" Mr.
Proctor pushes. "Can you please just catch me up?" Dennis
says tiredly. The Zoom room becomes tense. He sees some
students widen their eyes and keep quiet. He sees others
start to laugh. Ishmael, the class clown, writes in the chat.

Ishmael to Everyone

 LOL Dennis always getting into
trouble in the morning

"Stay on the call after class is over, Mr. Edu."

Who does he think he is? Dennis wants to say, but doesn't
want to make more trouble. Everyone knows Mr. Proctor
is strict and Dennis challenges him.

"Today, we're going to talk about the Enlightenment thinkers: John Locke, Charles Montesquieu, and Thomas Hobbes," Mr. Proctor says excitedly.

"In other words, some racist-ass dead white men," Dennis mumbles under his breath. The class snickers.

"Dennis," Proctor says sharply. "Again, I will see you after class." He continues, "These are *philosophers* who traveled all around the world and gathered information about how different countries governed their people. They brought their findings back to England and France to shape their own government. Their work is seen today in the United States Constitution."

Dennis thinks about how many people contributed to this country, but still don't have a place in the constitution. He thinks about his neighbor, Mr. Bio, the unhoused Vietnam vet who sleeps on New York Ave, and still can't meet his basic human needs. He thinks about his mother, a health worker during a pandemic, fighting for the health of this country's citizens, when she is not yet one herself. He thinks about himself, someone who wants to live "The American Dream," but is stopped by the simple fact that he is not American.

Mr. Proctor continues, "Now, America is in the middle of a scary time, and an important election that will determine the fate of this land. I'm sure you all feel the suspense, especially as many of you are not able to vote yet."

Trust me, I know, Dennis thinks.

"For this reason, I'm giving you an essay assignment.

I want you to answer the question, 'What does democracy mean to you?' in a three-page paper. I will collect them Monday, November 2nd."

"The day before the election? Oh, you trippin' Mr. P," Ishmael says.

"The purpose of this is for you to be inspired by the election. Consider this essay your vote."

After Mr. Proctor dismisses the students, Dennis immediately exits the Zoom to avoid his scolding.

That night, a notification pops up on Dennis' phone. It's an email from Mr. Procter, addressed to his mom, with the principal cc'ed.

Mr. Proctor

to Dennis, Ms. Edu, Principal Chuku

Dear Ms. Edu,

My name is Mr. Proctor and I am a teacher at your son's school. I am writing to let you know your son's behavior recently has warranted me to seek your help. Dennis always goes back and forth with me thereby not letting me be able to teach. He makes jokes in class which gives other students an excuse to lose their focus. Now, I understand he is just a teenager, which is why I have tried to get through to him. Today, for example, he arrived late and used profanity to distract the class. I asked for him to stay after class so we could figure out a way to move forward. After class he left before we could speak. If it is possible, I would like to talk more about this topic with you and Dennis on Zoom. All I ask for is 15-30 minutes of your time so that I can remind Dennis of the expectations of my class.

Please let me know a date and time that works best with your schedule.

Thank you for your time and I look forward to speaking soon,

Mr. Proctor

"Dennis! Dennis!! Dennis Emmanuel Edu!!!" Dennis' mom calls out from the kitchen. She's home early tonight, and clearly she just got the same news.

"Yes, Mom!" Dennis screams from his room.

"Come downstairs and explain this email," she says.

Dennis runs down the stairs. He knows not to play with his mom when she calls out his full name.

"It's really nothing, Mom. The man is just always on my case," Dennis says in defense.

"Did you go back and forth with him, disrupting his class?" his mom asks.

"I didn't mean for it to go like that."

"Since when are you the bad child, Dennis? You have dreams, a bright future ahead of you."

"Yes, but how will I achieve that if I can't even get a job to help you?"

Dennis' mom drops the kitchen knife in the sink and washes her hands. She makes her way to the couch, and taps the spot next to her, signaling him to sit down.

"Listen, I know you're going through a lot — with missing your father, with you changing schools this year, with graduation around the corner. Yes, it is not ideal, but you have to remain focused. The American Dream may not be what you expected, but *your* dreams are real, son. *That* is what your father and I want for you. Don't think about me. I am your mother; it is my job to provide for you, and as long as you remain my son, I will always worry and provide in any way I can."

Dennis hears her, but he doesn't believe her. He thinks of the last words his father ever said to him: *You are the man of the house now. Take care of your mother.*

"You just don't understand!" he yells, and makes his way back to his room.

His mom raises her eyebrows and widens her eyes, but says nothing. She shakes her head, turns her back and returns to making a dinner that Dennis won't eat.

Once Dennis slams the door shut, he puts on his earphones. Jazz always calms him down. Tonight, Robert Glasper's *Black Radio*. He opens his computer, opens a Word document, types WHAT DEMOCRACY MEANS TO ME... and stares at the blank page.

Wednesday, October 28, 2020

When Dennis wakes up, he's hungry... STARVING. He runs downstairs and is surprised to see his mom sitting at the kitchen table in front of her laptop.

"Good morning," he says as if nothing happened the night before.

His mom says nothing.

"Mom, I said 'good morning,'" this time, a little louder.

"I took the morning off from work. We have a meeting with Mr. Proctor," she says coldly.

Dennis doesn't respond. He grabs the box of granola bars from the top of the kitchen cabinet. He sits right next to his mother, but it is the furthest they've ever felt from each other. He taps his fingers to kill the awkward silence. It doesn't work.

All of a sudden, they hear a doorbell tone coming from the computer. Mr. Proctor's face appears on the screen, his bald head as shiny as ever, his goatee neatly trimmed, thin-framed glasses resting at the bottom of his nose.

"Hi! Ms. Edu, it is nice to finally meet you!"

"Oh! You can call me Grace!"

"Alright then, Ms. Grace."

Dennis put his hand on his forehead. *Bro, why is he always so proper?*

"Nice to meet you as well... though, I wish it were under better circumstances." She pinches Dennis' leg underneath the table. "Say *hi*," she whispers.

"Morning," Dennis says, knowing this isn't gonna be good.

"*Good* morning, Mr. Edu. And thank you, Ms. Grace, for taking the time out of your day to have this meeting and for making sure that Dennis shows up. Dennis, from what I've both seen and heard, you have always been a good student. Your past grades have been excellent. In fact, you have never gotten anything lower than a B+."

Nervous about where this is going, Dennis grabs a pencil and begins to hum, making a mellow beat in his head in an effort to tune him out.

Mr. Proctor continues, "My colleagues at the school Dennis attended last year also told me how respectful he was, how he always helped out during and after class, and even encouraged his classmates to do better. However, that has not been the case in *this* school, and ESPECIALLY in my class."

"Bruhhh," Dennis says.

Dennis' mom grabs Dennis' hand to stop him from speaking. She brings her other palm to her forehead, and shakes her head in disbelief.

Mr. Proctor goes on, "Now, I do think this young man has enormous potential, and each time I have offered my help, it has been thrown back at my face. He disrupts my teaching, makes jokes about how shiny my bald head is, and challenges me in front of the other students. Do you have any insight into why Dennis is behaving like this?"

Dennis' mother waits for what feels like a lifetime

before she responds.

"First, I would like to say thank you, Mr. Proctor, for bringing this situation to my attention and for investing in my son's future. At his old school, Dennis had limited opportunities, so we moved to this one for its elite college-readiness program for immigrant students. But recently Dennis has been struggling. He's been stuck on achieving success ever since coming to the United States. In the past, he always handled the pressure in his own way, so I thought nothing of it. But with the election coming up, I've caught him looking at the news a lot. I think he's worried about what his immigration status means for his future."

Dennis listens to his mother's accent as she tries to explain his behavior. Her words are thick, but soft, English, with a hint of Nigeria still stubborn on her tongue.

Listening to her makes him think about his essay. *Does democracy allow the contradictions that his mother's voice holds? That all immigrant voices hold?*

Mr. Proctor interrupts him as he meditates on these questions. "Mr. Edu, is there anything you have to say for yourself?"

Dennis doesn't feel like talking. "What do you want from me?" he says.

"Well, what do you want for yourself?" Mr. Proctor asks. "Because I don't think you are on the path to get it."

Dennis balls his fists, and puts enough bass in his voice to sound like his father.

"Don't you have other students to antagonize? The 'right

path' requires no obstacle. And look at me! I'm a 17-year-old Black immigrant who can't get a job because my citizenship hangs in the balance between two old white men! And I need to be the man of the house. Dad always said—"

"Your father is dead, Dennis. You need to learn how to be your own man," his mother says.

His mother says this out loud and the wall that Dennis built up comes shattering down. This is the first time that his mother has acknowledged his father's death. The first time she isn't allowing Dennis to deny it. He can no longer pretend that it isn't true.

"I've watched you act like this wasn't a reality ever since he got the tumor, but it has been one year. You can't keep living like this. Your father would want you to—"

Dennis slams the table with both fists.

"Dennis, calm down. I know you have a lot of emotions right now, but—" Mr. Proctor starts.

"I'm not going to sit here and take advice from people who don't understand me."

Dennis hastily grabs his phone, charger, and book bag, and heads for the front door. He pauses for a second to think if he is really about to do what he's going to do. Still… he decides to leave.

Thursday, October 29, 2020

Dennis wakes up on a bench in Chuck Brown Memorial Park. *Good thing I had my hoodie in my bag*, Dennis thinks. He decided to sleep there because it is a place where he always felt serene. When he arrived in DC and started exploring his neighborhood, he happened upon it, and thought it was magical. Music, even Go-Go, has always felt like home. Not to mention, Woodbridge Library right up the street. Even though they're operating on a modified schedule, not even opening until 11:00 a.m., he could still use their Wi-Fi to attend his virtual classes.

Angry, scared, confused, and hurt, Dennis still feels these emotions kick at him from inside his chest. It almost dizzies him, but he looks at his phone. 8:00 a.m. Time for school.

Dennis makes his way to the library and sits on the ground, against the stone-walled entrance. He connects his phone to an outdoor outlet and logs into Mr. Proctor's class. Camera off.

A private message appears on the screen:

Mr. Proctor to Dennis (Private Message)

M   **Are you ok?**

Dennis to Mr. Proctor (Private Message)

D   **I'm fine**

Mr. Proctor to Dennis (Private Message)

 Your mother is looking for you. She's worried sick.

Dennis doesn't respond. He continues his research for the big paper, counting down the hours until he'll be allowed inside the warm building.

Friday, October 30, 2020

It's 6:00 a.m. The cold wakes Dennis up on the same
bench where he slept the night before. On the bench next
to him, he sees a man drinking dark brown liquid out
of a beat-up water bottle. The man hums a sad tune and
nods in and out. He looks at Dennis, but says nothing.
Behind him, an old barefoot lady walks around in circles.
He becomes anxious being around people who he doesn't
know. He wonders if his new neighbors are as lonely as he
is, or lonelier. He sees their suffering... *Democracy is not for
all I guess,* he thinks, but then realizes that he actually has
a home to return to... if he wanted. Dennis feels shame,
but locks it in a cage and throws it into the darkest place
in his heart, along with the rest of the feelings he denies.
He shakes his head and decides to wait at the library door.

Dennis contemplates his decision to run away. He
knew his mother would be worried, but she'd also be too
scared to call the cops on her Black, immigrant son. What
he was doing was unfair. *Maybe, democracy is selfish... just
like me,* Dennis thinks. For two days, he's been surviving
on a pack of granola bars that he keeps in his backpack just
in case, and at night there are bugs trying to munch on
him like he is some tasty burrito. *Is all of this worth it?*

Today, when he logs onto class, he feels tired and
depressed. He feels so bombarded with emotions, that
for the first five minutes of class, he forgets to turn his
camera off.

His heart drops to his stomach. *I hope that Mr. Proctor didn't notice,* Dennis thinks. But for the rest of class, Mr. Proctor says nothing to him, and Dennis starts to calm down.

Man! That was a close one.

Today, Dennis stays in the library until it closes at 7:00 p.m.

When he walks outside, towards the same bench where he slept the night before, and the night before that, he feels breath at the back of his neck. Dennis tries to turn around and *BOOM!* Someone punches his right eye, grabs his bag, and takes off. Dennis runs after the figure — after the bag that has become his only home — but can't catch up. Dennis watches the figure fade into darkness…

Just then, a car swerves into the library lot, and begins to follow Dennis. *What now?!* Dennis thinks.

The driver rolls down his window. "DENNIS!" A familiar voice yells.

Dennis turns around in shock, "Mr. Proctor?! What are you doing here?"

"Get in, Mr. Edu. Let's have a chat," he says, handing Dennis a Black KN9 mask that matches his own.

Dennis sighs, takes the mask and puts it on, before reluctantly opening the door. He sits down on the ripped cloth of Mr. Proctor's front seat.

"What's up, Mr. Proctor?" Dennis asks, still holding onto his pride, not wanting Mr. Proctor to see how he regrets running away from home, from his mom, and all the pain emotionally… and physically.

He rubs the swollen knot of his right eye.

"Look man, I don't know how long you're planning on staying out here, and, by the looks of it, you're not doing okay…" Mr. Proctor hands him a cold Coke bottle. "This should help with the swelling."

"Thank you," Dennis mumbles, placing the Coke against his face.

"Mr. Edu, your mother has been worried sick. I've been worried too. Have you been sleeping outside the library for the past two days?"

"Mr. Proctor, here's the thing: nobody around me understands what I am going through because they have never been in my shoes. Not you, not my mom, nobody! I'm about to graduate, and my green card application has been pending ever since the pandemic started. I can't even get a job — not a good one. How am I supposed to support my mom, to be the man of the house, like my father told me to? Instead, I'm just a burden. Trying to understand my predicament is like pouring water on stone. So please if you would just let me out of your car before I scream that you kidnapped me, that would be great."

"Whoa! It's 8:00 p.m., It's cold outside, you have no blanket, no food. And I know that because your stomach has been growling ever since you got into my car. And

I mean, look at your face! Look at your clothes! Not to mention, you're stinking up my car like a wet dog because I'm guessing you haven't showered in days. I am here to help you... if you can believe that."

Dennis wants to believe Mr. Proctor, so he stays, settles into the warm car seat, and sees what else he has to say.

Mr. Proctor takes both of his arms off the steering wheel, seemingly releasing all the tension he typically holds. Dennis sees a vulnerability that he hasn't seen before.

"Dennis," Mr. Proctor begins softly, "for the most part, your main problem seems to be people not understanding you, is that right?"

Dennis nods slowly.

"Well, what if *I* do? What if I told you I am originally from a small village in Kenya? Never knew my dad. Never knew my mom."

Dennis sits upright.

"I was an orphan who happened to win a visa lottery by the age of 20. I came to this country with no sense of direction — I know what it means to have to grow up quickly. Knowing how this country treats people who look like us, sound like us, I even felt pressured to erase my accent just to get a job."

He shifts in his seat.

"We have gone through the hardest thing a young adult starting up can go through. You said during the meeting with your mother that your father told you you needed to be the man of the house. But how would you know what's right or wrong unless you let other people try to help you? Being a man takes a village."

Tears drop down Dennis' cheeks.

"So yes, you want to help your mom and further your future, however you also need to believe in yourself and live your life, knowing your father lives on through you! Count your blessings: your mother is here for you, I am here for you. You have a home, food, and a warm bed. Not everyone has that, man." Mr. Proctor nudges Dennis' shoulder playfully and Dennis smiles.

Mr. Proctor then smells his hand and scrunches his nose. "Man, now my hand stinks. Let's get you home so that you can bathe, Mr. Edu."

"Ahh, now you're back to your uptight self." They both laugh. "Yeah, yeah, let's go home."

Mr. Proctor pulls up to the Edu's front porch and turns off the car. "You ready?" Mr. Proctor asks, while opening the car door.

"I am," Dennis says with straightened posture and a newfound sense of peace. They walk up to the front door, but Dennis' mother swings it open before they could even touch the knob.

She covers her mouth with her palm, and embraces Dennis so tightly that even Mr. Proctor hears his bones crack.

"Where did you find him?" she sobs.

"I'll get to that later. For now, I'll let you two have this moment," he says, patting Dennis' shoulder before walking back to his car.

Now, with the two finally alone, Dennis cries, "I am so sorry, Mom. We got a lot to talk about."

"I know. Come eat first."

His mother leans her head on Dennis' shoulder, holds his waist, and walks with him to the kitchen.

Weekend, October 31 – November 1, 2020

Over the next few days, Dennis feels grateful, appreciating what he has rather than mourning the things he doesn't. In fact, the entire Edu household feels more optimistic about the future, even as the country seems to grow more anxious.

Scrolling through his Twitter, he watches senators, tech CEOs, rappers, and even athletes cast their predictions about the election. But Dennis decides to avoid the negative energy and turns off his phone.

Dennis' mom took the weekend off to stay with her "little delinquent," as she started calling him since he returned. They talk about how they're going to move forward no matter what, about how it is necessary to ask for assistance when you're struggling. They talk about Dennis' father for the first time in a year, crying and laughing, and laughing, and laughing.

In the evenings, Dennis brings out his notebook, writing down his thoughts for the big essay he has due Monday morning. Though before he was stuck on how to explain democracy, not knowing how he fit inside of it, the words now seem to flow effortlessly. Dennis now knows what democracy means to him.

Monday, November 2, 2020

Monday morning. In class, even bone-headed Ishmael can't seem to stop talking about the election, trading in his punchlines to be the class' Fox5 News reporter.

Mr. Proctor sits back and carefully listens to students discuss what the election outcome might be and what it means for them. He doesn't judge their opinions, but occasionally prompts students with questions that may challenge their beliefs.

Before, when Dennis was in class, he dismissed Mr. Proctor, thinking he was just another person who didn't understand him. Now, watching Mr. Proctor's grace as he lets students process what's happening in this country, and witnessing his vulnerability as he opened up about his past troubles the night before, he sees his empathy. He sees his strength.

Dennis thinks about how, if Mr. Proctor hadn't found him, he himself wouldn't have the strength to face tomorrow, and the many tomorrows after that.

"Alright, students," Mr. Proctor says, "it is time to read your essays to the class on what democracy means to you. Who wants to go first?"" Everyone in the class seems to look away, put their heads down, or pretend to be distracted, until...

Dennis raises his hand.

"Mr. Edu, wow! Today must be a special day," he says with a proud smirk.

Dennis unmutes his computer, clears his throat:

"Is democracy for all? Or is it selfish? Does democracy allow for the contradictions that my mother's voice holds, that all immigrant voices hold?" he begins, with a steady heart. "Even I, who came to the United States from Enugu, Nigeria when I was 14 years old for the American Dream, never felt like the American Dream wanted *me*. But I recently learned with the help of someone who's been in my shoes before that democracy isn't lonely. Democracy is in community. In all of us. All of our voices and stories being heard…"

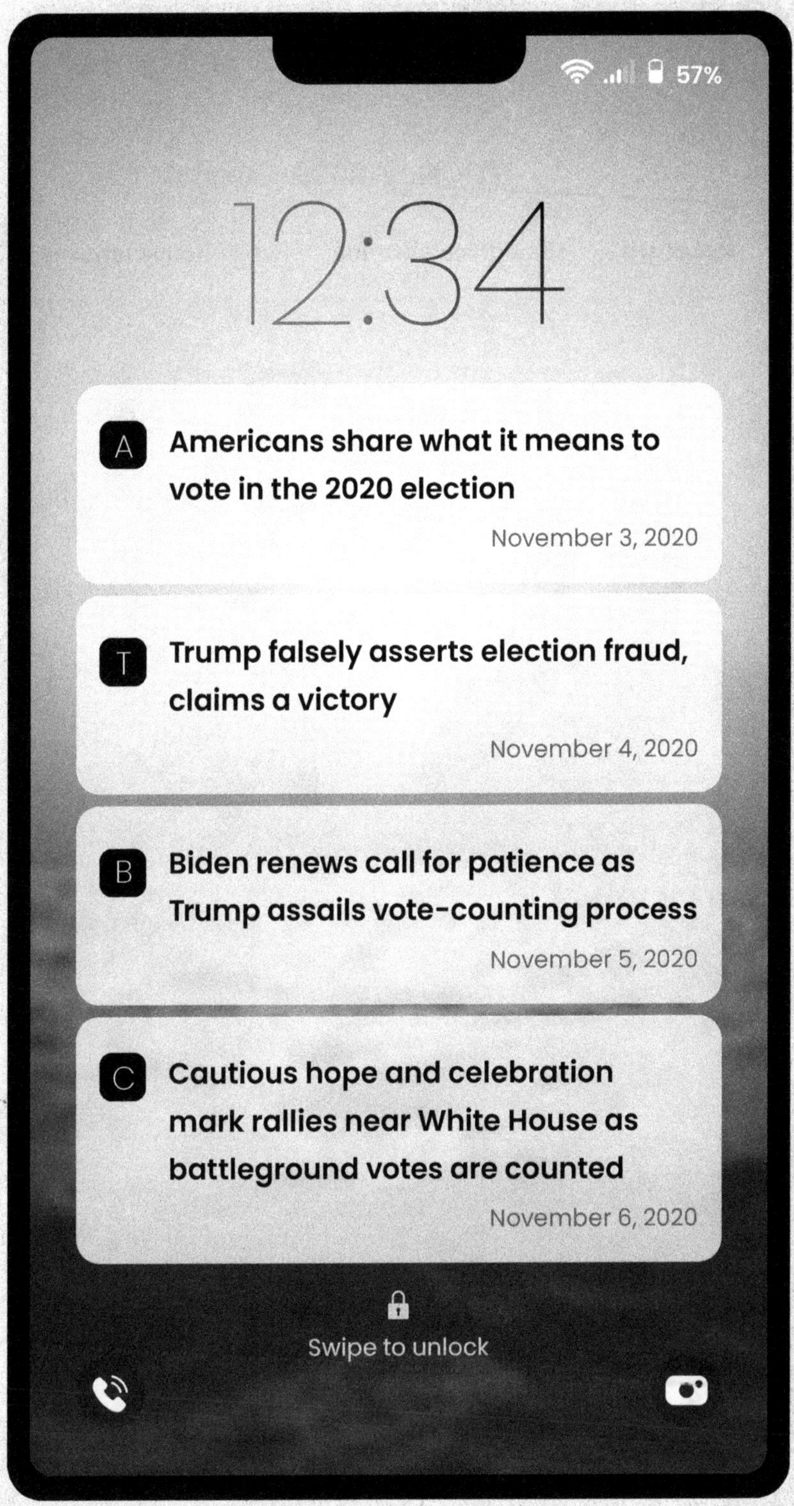
57%
12:34
A
Americans share what it means to vote in the 2020 election
November 3, 2020
T
Trump falsely asserts election fraud, claims a victory
November 4, 2020
B
Biden renews call for patience as Trump assails vote-counting process
November 5, 2020
C
Cautious hope and celebration mark rallies near White House as battleground votes are counted
November 6, 2020
Swipe to unlock

BLM plaza   election celebration   white house fence

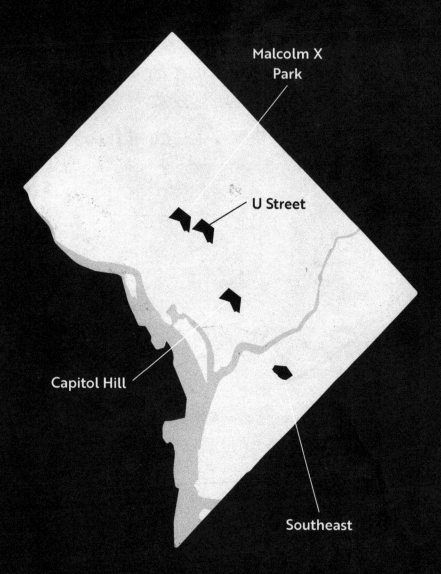

Malcolm X
Park

U Street

Capitol Hill

Southeast

WINTER

THE THINGS WE DO NOT SPEAK

by Najae Purvis

Najiy Shabazz

My name is Najiy, but they call me Jiy (G) where I'm from.
I've been called Jiy my whole life, to the point some people
don't even know my real name. I'm from Washington,
DC, where the president stays. I'm specifically from the
south side — Southeast — where it's known to be the
most dangerous part of the city. I live in this small, hectic
three-bedroom apartment. It's just me, my dad, and my
little sister. It's been just us for years. My mom died when I
was just one, and my sister's mom is nowhere to be found.
It's not always easy living in a single parent household. My
dad is always running around trying to figure everything
out with no help. It's hard to watch him struggle.

I attend one of the best high schools in the city, even

though I come from where I do. I used to travel forty-five minutes to school every day, back when we went to school in person. My dad is big on education and making sure we have a good life. I'm one person at home, and another person at school. School — it's a whole different world for me. White kids walking around every day, freedom, different slang. My high school had the smartest, brightest students around the city under one roof. It has been a struggle having to deal with 75% of the class being teachers' pets. And everyone being baby Einsteins. I've been in school for three years now, and it's finally my senior year. I don't know how I got through it, to be honest. School has been more challenging than ever before. Maybe it's my dyslexia, the change of environment, this pandemic... Or maybe it's my best friend.

I don't know.

c

That Dream

Ring Ring Ring Ring Ringggg

I'm walking and I see an abandoned payphone. It's ringing. I look around and it seems really empty. I walk towards the phone and pick it up. I don't know why I answer, I just do.

The phone's silent for a long pause, then I hear someone sniffle. Finally, they speak:

"Hellooo, is this Najiy Shabazz?"

The voice on the phone sounds just like Jada. No, Cam. Or maybe it's Kayla. I know sweet old Nyah wouldn't do this.

"Who's playing on my phone? This ain't funny."

Normally I don't mind a little laugh, but this moment doesn't seem like a joke. Things seem off. I don't hear any giggling in the background. And I didn't give anyone this number. The lights around me go out, and it's almost pitch black.

"Did Tray send you?" I ask. This is something he would do. Tray is my best friend — he is the funniest person I know — but he doesn't always know when he's taking a prank too far.

"I'm so sorry to tell you, but—"

Then it hits me — it sounds like Tray's aunt, Daysha. I pause. Why would she be calling me?

My heart drops to my feet. My brain begins to scrabble. About a hundred different scenarios play in my head, all at once...

And then, before she can say another word, I hang up.

I hang up hard.

I start to walk away, and then to run. Out of nowhere a basketball court pops up in front of me. It's the court we were just playing at the other day. Tray running down the court to shoot. He makes it of course — doesn't he seem okay? Cool? — and everyone cheers him on. But suddenly he stops. He stares at me.

I don't know what's going on.

We look at each other for a long time. And then, his eyes widen. His face starts to turn red. The veins in his throat pop out, and he screams like a baby crying out to his mommy.

Help.

Denial

Monday, December 21, 2020 — morning

I wake up sweaty and breathing heavy. My heart's beating fast and my throat feels tight. I know it was That Dream. The one I've been having all month. I don't know what I can do to escape it. I watch movies every night before bed — from scary ones to cartoons — hoping I'll dream about that stuff instead. Last night, I watched *Space Jam*, hoping I would dream about playing with Michael Jordan. But no.

I shake off the nightmare, then stretch my body to make sure that I am fully awake. Then I head straight to my sister, Angel's room. Every day, I make sure that she gets up so my dad can sleep in. He works late every night, and rarely gets rest. She complains every time, begging me to let her sleep a little more. She slowly rolls off the bed and sits there with her eyes closed. I shake her a little, tell her to hurry up. Eventually, my sister gets dressed, and she gets started on her virtual day.

I head to the kitchen and make us some French toast, bacon, and eggs with some orange juice. Since I am the only morning person here, I like to be helpful and productive. When I get things done, it makes me feel good. It helps me stay positive and block out bad feelings… like my dream.

I give Angel her plate and then wake up my dad. I check the clock, and it's already 9:20. My class starts at 9:30, and I don't even know where my computer is. I rush to my room and rip it apart. My room is so little, but still it's nowhere to be found. I look through my closet, I look under my bed with my art supplies. I look in all my different bags, and still nothing. After five long minutes — the clock ticking down to my class start-time — I find it. It's sitting on my bed, right under my pillow. I forgot that I was up the night before attempting to do work (that is, until I started watching a movie instead). I let out a loud sigh, log into the computer, and start my day.

Friends

Monday, December 21, 2020 — afternoon

After school, Jada, Cam, and I link up at my girlfriend Kayla's house for our "study session." We meet once a week in Kayla's basement, for about two hours. Some of our parents were nervous about us meeting at first. But the isolation is TOO MUCH — we couldn't go a whole year without seeing each other. So our parents finally gave in. Well, everyone except Tray's family. Tray could never come. His aunt was too worried about him getting the babies sick, even though we all wore masks. It hurts to think about that. So especially now, we make the time to catch up, just be together.

Today, since there's only one more day before winter break, we don't stress about work. We take our papers out, but we don't even look at them. We're distracted, talking about our winter break plans. Well, really *their* winter break plans.

"I forgot to tell you guys but — I'm so excited — I got that internship with the IT program! I might be able to keep doing it during college," Cam says.

"Oh that's great!" Jada hugs him.

Kayla has a big grin and says, "I'm so happy you got it!"

"You know me, I'll probably be working all winter break," Jada says.

"Yea girl, we know you don't play about your money," Kayla teases her.

"Let me borrow some," I say, and we all laugh together.

Kayla tells us about her grandparents coming into town and how much she misses them. Her family's from Texas and she doesn't get to see them much. Everyone has plans except me. It kind of sucks that I can't do anything. My dad isn't going to allow me to see my mom's side of the family this year because of COVID. And he won't let me get a job either. My friends will all be busy. And my best friend… isn't here. The only real time when I get a break — I have nothing and no one.

"What about you, Jiy?" Kayla asks.

"Uuuum… I don't know," I say. I stumble, trying to think of something actually worth saying. "I might play a little basketball. I might see Uncle Mark."

My friends smile in that way that's kind but also pitying. I'm wondering when people will stop looking at me that way.

I finally look at my phone and it's already 8:00 p.m. The time goes fast when we're not doing work. I can't lie, I'm a little sad that I won't be seeing them until January. But at least Kayla and I can see each other every day.

Kayla

Kayla and I aren't the typical couple — we share a friend group. We only live five minutes apart, so it's easy to hang out. All we usually do is play games, and watch movies together. Kayla's favorite genre is horror, and she is always trying to convince me to watch that stuff. I am more of a rom-com guy — I like to sympathize with what characters are going through. Watching horror does nothing but make me look like a punk.

For a while I would try to meet her half-way and watch the funny-scary ones. But that took away the point of it actually being horror, because we would just be laughing. Kayla didn't mind that though. She saw my efforts and appreciated that at least I tried.

Even though we all hung out, the guys would still make sure to do 'guy' things. We talk about sports highlights and make bets, we play 2K and talk about girls. The guys used to get mad that I spent so much time with Kayla. They said that I never really got on the game party chats anymore. Or that I didn't come to the court that much. Tray wasn't with it at all. He would tell me, "She can't take all the love, Bro. What about me??"

We just laughed it off. Continued on with our day.

The Text
Tuesday, December 22, 2020

When I log out on Tuesday afternoon, ready to head into
twelve whole days of winter break, I'm feeling good. I need
a break. I know I'm gonna be bored, but at least I finally
have time to relax and focus on self-care. I also know I've
been busy these past few weeks, so I just hope that without
all that I won't come crashing down.

That night I'm in the kitchen, making some spaghetti
for my family, when Angel runs up to me with my phone.

"Here, KayKay called you like five times."

I text her, asking if anything's wrong. I'll call her back
after I finish making all the food.

Kayla texts back. She says that she has a headache, sore
throat, and chills. I immediately call her. She texts to say
call back later — she's next in line to get a COVID test.

I just saw her yesterday. My heart instantly drops.
What happens if I get COVID? Or give it to my family? I
can't think about that right now. I have to stay positive. It's
probably just a cold. I finish making the spaghetti and give
Angel a plate.

While Angel eats, I sit at the table and look up all the
COVID symptoms that one can have. Half these things
I always have. Tiredness. Shortness of breath. Diarrhea.
Runny nose. Reading all these symptoms makes me not
even hungry any more.

I don't know whether I should go ahead and isolate

myself or just try to get tested. I don't know what to do. My body goes into straight panic-mode. It's almost as if I'm frozen by my anxieties. *Let me give myself a minute to calm down*, I think. *Maybe this whole thing will just blow over.*

Kayla

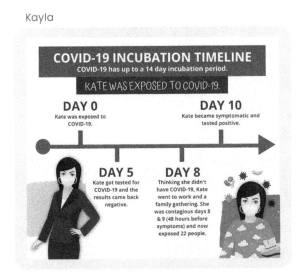

Waiting
Thursday, December 24, 2020 — morning

It's Thursday — two days later — and Kayla still hasn't gotten her test results back. It's also Christmas Eve. Ugh. I have to stay in my room in case I'm carrying the virus. It's weird to feel like a ticking time bomb — will I get sick too? I'm trying to stay positive through this whole waiting process. I am hoping for the best, but I would rather be safe than sorry.

I've been working on small-side hobbies to keep myself busy: drawing, making posters, doing crafts for my room. I even made a little net on my door with a trash can underneath to shoot my trash. I'm trying to exercise a little and practice my meditation, too. It just won't work out for me, though — I can't do it for more than like five minutes. I zone out as soon as the workout gets intense or the meditation gets boring.

I'm trying to use this time to find my true passion. I honestly don't know what I like. I haven't really noticed 'til now that there aren't many things for me in this world. The only things I actually like are basketball and my friends. Art and creativity make me happy, but… it's just been too hard these past few weeks. Art can make you go deep, and that's the last place I want to be.

I'm also trying to stick to my routines, or at least the stuff I can still do while isolating. Angel and I decided that we would FaceTime and eat breakfast together in different rooms. Dad makes us toast and eggs and leaves mine outside my door. Angel gets her tablet, props it up, and starts rambling about her day. It helps me feel like I have some control, but I can't help thinking about what I could be doing if it wasn't for COVID. This is winter break, a time that's supposed to be fun, full of relaxing and visiting people. But instead I'm stuck in this room, waiting.

Exposed

Thursday, December 24, 2020 — evening

It's late that evening when I get the text: Kayla's positive. I
immediately let out a huge gasp, and my throat closes up.
Is it because of COVID or anxiety? I've been asking myself
that question a lot lately. I text Dad to let him know the
news. I feel terrible — it's the holidays and instead of
bringing gifts, I'm bringing sickness. I don't know for
sure, but there is a likely chance at least. I was with Kayla
almost every day leading up to her getting sick. I feel bad
for little Angel. She can't even go play with the kids her
age. She has to be stuck in this house with us. I can't play
dolls with her. I can't do anything. Dad can't go to work,
and Kayla won't text me back. It's like I've ruined things
for everyone.

The past couple of days, Kayla and I have been going
through some serious drama. She feels like we don't talk
enough — like I don't "open up to her" — and I feel like
she is just making things up. This is the longest me and
her have ever gone without seeing each other. We usually
see each other every day, at least on Zoom in class or at
lunch break, or in person at the study session or at the
park. But lately, we can't seem to get along. It's like we
argue every day, about the littlest things. Yesterday, we
argued about me not giving her a straight-up answer about
whether I was going to play my game that night. I mean,
I didn't think it's that serious — I just didn't know yet. If

she would have just straight-up said she wanted to be on the phone instead, that would have been okay. But instead she wanted to question me... It's like I miss her so much, but I can't stand to keep bickering.

On top of that, I have no one else to talk to. My friends are all busy — even though they were all at the "study session" too, they're not even isolating. Their families don't have health risks, so they are like, *Whatever happens, happens.* I don't blame them in a way. This is brutal. I honestly don't know if I'm going to be able to last a whole ten days here. It's only Day 2, and I feel so alone right now. The only thing I can look forward to is Angel eating breakfast with me on the other side of the door. How am I going to do this?

Isolation Day 3 — Christmas
Friday, December 25, 2020

Today it's Christmas. The worst Christmas ever. I won't be
able to see my family and friends. I won't get a chance to
see Aunt Christine and the baby. I won't get to try Aunt
Shernice's Christmas ham (it's always the best thing about
the meal.) Dad's making a special dinner but it just won't
hit the same. He doesn't cook as well as the women in
the family. I won't see Uncle Mark, and the holidays are
the only time we see him now. He was my favorite uncle,
but he just got up and moved away. He was supposed
to drive down for a few days but now he can't because I
was exposed. It's like I will never really get to crack jokes
and spend time with him anymore. And Cousin Tia? She
always has the best gifts, and the most kids. I can't believe
I won't see them this year. I enjoy listening to all four of
her kids argue about nothing. They're so funny — every
year we are all entertained, except Tia. I honestly don't
know how she deals with it 25/8. Cousin Mary is still at
college in Maryland — she was supposed to come by but
now she's not. I was really looking forward to her telling
me what it was like at her college.

I can't help but feel bad for Dad and Angel. They have
no one either. Even though I've been in quarantine, no one
wants to be around the guy with the sick kid. And now I
put Angel at risk with her health. We all have something
that puts us more at-risk than average. Dad has diabetes

and struggles with eating. Angel and I both have asthma. Dad has been racking up on vitamin C and making sure we stay hydrated. I feel guilty for exposing them. Angel struggles a little bit more with her asthma — she has a special machine she uses sometimes. I can't stand to think about her in bed all day, coughing and not being able to go outside. All she wanted to do was run in the grass and be a normal kid. I would never want to see her in pain. I can't lose her too.

Like I said: Worst. Christmas. Ever.

Isolation Day 6
Monday, December 28, 2020

Still no symptoms. Every morning, I think I'm going to wake up with a sore throat. Or the headache. Or the stuffy nose. But nothing. I probably should have gotten tested but I just couldn't deal. Those lines were long and it was cold. And now, maybe I don't even wanna know.

This loneliness is driving me a little crazy. I stopped eating breakfast with Angel. I stopped even getting out of bed. I barely even talk to any of my friends anymore. What's the point? I feel like I'm losing myself.

The problem started when I began to let myself think. I couldn't avoid it anymore. I would put on my slow jams and think about the good old days. Back when the group was all tight, and nobody could tell us nothing. We were like the six musketeers, if that was a thing. We would be with each other every day. One person was in trouble, and we all were there. Someone's family event? We all were there. When somebody felt down or blue? We all were there.

I can't lie, it's hard not to think about the good old days...

Back in the Day — Sophomore Year

"Alright class, get in groups and start the lab," the teacher yelled out.

"Hey, do you guys wanna ask that dude over there if he wants to be in a group with us?" Cam pointed at a kid sitting in the corner alone. He had on this cool black and blue hoodie. And we had the same Air Forces on.

"Yeah sure, why not," I replied. He seemed cool.

Cam walked over to where the boy was sitting. "Hey dude, you want to work with us?" Cam asked.

He looked over at us and nodded, a little nervous. "Sure."

"Okay, cool, we need a fourth."

The tall boy got up, got a chair, and pulled it up to us.

"Wassup," I said. "My name is Najiy, what's your name?"

"Heyy Najiy, I'm Tray. Nice to meet y'all."

For this lab, we needed to create some sort of cardboard box contraption that would keep a substance safe and prevent it from getting cold. We started off by brainstorming different ideas. Then we began to make sketches and notes about what we were going to do. We decided to focus on structure. Tray wanted to include cushions, warm fabric, and good spacing. He was smart like that.

Mr. Petty wanted us to use an egg for our trial to make sure our box was effective. Tray was like, "The ancestors must have known he was gonna be petty, to

make that his last name." Then he kept making these
weird egg jokes, like, "What did the egg say after it was
ghosted? Why are you egg-noring me?"

Me and Tray were in charge of all the technical stuff,
and everybody else wanted to design the box and make it
look pretty. Tray and I started talking while we worked on
it. I could tell instantly that this guy got me. He was super-
focused, but also goofy. I couldn't help but let out a laugh
when he talked in his serious voice. It seemed as if even his
playful side was serious.

After a few days of goofing off in lab, he showed me
his poetry and I showed him my art. Then we started
talking about sports. We showed each other our clips from
games. He actually was pretty good, but not better than
me of course.

He brought our group together, to be honest. We had
all been lab partners for a month already, but it wasn't
until we met Tray that we finally made a group chat. It
wasn't until we met Tray that we felt complete.

Tray

Of the whole group, Tray and I became the closest. We texted every day and went to the court together. We were always there for each other when one of us needed to rant. He understood when I got frustrated at the world, when I felt like I couldn't be understood.

At the end of sophomore year, I was so anxious about my grades that I didn't even want to look when we got our grades back from this one teacher. I'd been struggling in her class all year. *I hope I pass, but who knows,* I thought. The teacher placed my paper on my desk upside-down and said, "You could have done better." Then she went to the next student. *What am I supposed to do with that? What does that even mean? Is she saying, I passed but it was low… or that I failed?* I didn't even look at the paper, I just quickly put it in my bookbag and walked out of the class.

Later that day, I went home and finally got up the courage to look. I failed. I'd never been so discouraged in my life. I felt so low and disappointed in myself. This meant that I would have to attend summer school. I couldn't believe I had thrown my whole summer away.

On my first day of summer school I got there early, so I was the first one in class. I was so upset. I just knew I had to do better. Other students slowly started coming in, and next thing you knew, a familiar face walked in — Tray! I tell you, my face lit up. I was so happy it didn't make any sense. I was just grateful that someone I knew was here with me. I wondered why neither one of us mentioned summer school to each other, but we were both private, and held ourselves to high standards. Maybe he was disappointed, too. We talked about how hard chemistry was, and how we wished to do better. With him there, the rest of class went by easy.

Me and Tray walked home together that day, and we talked about some deep stuff. I was telling him how I felt like a disappointment and never failed ever. He put me in my place fast. He let me know that everything happens for a reason. And that we wouldn't be in this situation if we weren't supposed to. Like, maybe we needed this summer, together?

From that day on, when I was feeling a little down, I would hit Tray up. We would stay on the phone for hours and hours. For once I felt heard, I felt understood. I decided he was gonna be the person I expressed myself to from then on. He made me look at life through a whole new lens. All summer we stuck together, and we worked hard, both passing the class with an A. I left that class with a best friend. I don't know what I would have done if it wasn't for him.

What will I do now?

That Dream Again
Wednesday, December 30, 2020 — before sunrise

Ring Ring Ring Ring Ringggg

I'm walking and I see an abandoned payphone. It's ringing. I look around and it seems really empty. I walk towards the phone and pick it up. I don't know why I answer, I just do.

The phone's silent for a long pause, then I hear someone sniffle. Finally, they speak:

"Hellooo, is this Najiy Shabazz?"

The voice is Tray's aunt. Not this dream again!

"I'm sorry to tell you, but—"

I hang up again. Walk away again. Run again. And this time, as the court appears, and Tray makes his shot, and then screams, this time I notice Tray isn't crying out for his mommy. He's calling out for me.

I wake up instantly.

Facing It, Part I
Wednesday, December 30, 2020

It's December 30th. That makes Day 8 of isolation, but honestly, it's the day I've been most afraid of this whole time, and it's got nothing to do with COVID.

It's the day of Tray's funeral.

You guessed it, didn't you? I knew it, too, but I've been running. For forty long days, I've been running and running away from it. I can't run anymore. My best friend is really gone, and I can't even be there to say goodbye.

I can't believe I'm missing his funeral. My heart turns into stone and cracks into a million pieces as it hits me. They could only invite ten people to the service, and I was one of them. That's how close me and Tray were. But obviously I couldn't go. Not while I was in isolation. I've been trying so hard to block it out, to not register that he was really gone, but it's only now that it's hitting me how selfish that is. It's only now I'm realizing that I'm not going to be there for him.

…And maybe I never was.

Because you want to know the real truth?

The truth is that my best friend Tray passed away from suicide. November 20, 2020. Right before Thanksgiving. Right after I saw him and thought everything was fine.

The fact that my best friend was going through things mentally and I had no idea is crazy. When I wasn't in a good place, he encouraged me to keep on going, he'd say "the storm eventually passes." But now when I think about it, he never really talked about anything too deep. He would just talk about simple teenage stuff. He never talked about what he was going through mentally. I remember that day he wanted to ball, and he was making jokes. *She can't take all the love, Bro. What about me?*

As I sit in bed and stalk his aunt's Facebook for pictures of the funeral, it plays in my head over and over. *...What about me?* I never realized that there was something deeper going on. The fact that he was calling out for my help all along, it genuinely hurts. I wonder if it will hurt this way all my life.

I can't take any more, so I close my laptop, close my eyes, and I do the only thing I can right now: I cry.

Facing It, Part II

I don't think I've been the same since I got that phone call. That was real, by the way — when his aunt called me, saying "I"m sorry to tell you, but—." She sounded so distraught and empty. That was the worst day of my life. It's just that it wasn't some creepy payphone like in that dream. That dream I kept having over and over.

Just the thought of his name makes me wanna throw up. My friends and I don't even say it. For the past month, we've avoided all subjects and conversations about him. It's like if we pretend he didn't exist then we won't have to talk about it. It worked for a while, but...

As much as we tried to take him out of the equation, I guess parts of me never fully healed. How could they? Everything changed when he left this earth. The one person who understood me is gone. I still can't believe it.

And worse, I can't believe he did it *himself.* I'm still trying to grasp the idea of suicide. One day I was reading the news on my phone, and it said that nearly 46,000 people took their own lives this year. Apparently, suicide was among the ten leading causes of death in 2020. I literally was with him almost everyday. How did I not notice that he was going to become one of those 46,000?

Tray must have felt like he had no one. He couldn't attend all the meet-ups, always had to babysit, didn't have time to ball. Tray was the type to always be there for his family. I never knew he felt some type of way. He would help his aunt without hesitation or complaints, and he did everything he could to protect his family's health. His aunt didn't want him to get his little cousins sick, and he loved them more than anything, so he just closed himself off from all possible harm.

I honestly don't know how he was handling all the stress of being in school and basically a part-time parent, during a pandemic. It must have been so overwhelming. I know it was for me, I didn't even think about how hard he had it. And mannn, his little cousins. It hurts me to think of their little faces. They looked up to him like a dad.

OK, It feels good to admit it. Well, not good, exactly. It hurts. But it's felt so heavy for so long to be carrying all of that, pretending it's not weighing me down. Now it's like, I finally cried about it, I finally let it out and I can start to breathe again.

Isolation Day 10 — New Year's Day
Friday, January 1, 2021

Today begins a new year. A new energy. I do feel a bit of a difference, and not just because it's my last day of quarantine and I never even got sick. For everybody, it's a day for starting over, looking ahead. It's still a hard time for me — pain doesn't just dissolve like that, even when you drown it in tears — but I do feel a new sense of purpose. I know I have to do things differently when I get out. I don't want to be that guy anymore. The guy who doesn't take things seriously. The guy who doesn't talk about his feelings. The guy who loses his best friend and doesn't cry. The guy who's lonely even before isolation. The guy who doesn't even know his own self.

I call Angel on her iPad and ask if we can eat breakfast together today. While we eat, I ask her what she got for Christmas (because no, I didn't even ask before.) She shows me her new skates and tells me that she's so excited she can't wait to use them.

"Maybe I'll take you to the court, and you can skate around when I go."

"Yea! I wanna go with you!"

"That's a deal!" I can't help but smile.

After my dad takes my plate, I decide to take advantage of my last day of isolation and do something I love. Try to get my head on right. I take out my canvas and paint from under my bed. I turn on some music and begin to sketch out this image of me and my friends on the court. This takes me back to my happy place, back when things were just so simple. Before big feelings, before death, before this virus. I feel like that was the last time we were together before our lives turned upside-down.

I stare at the painting for a while and realize something is off. How could we all have the same facial expression? We look too happy. Were we all hiding how we really felt deep down? Jada's family was struggling with bills, Cam was failing math, and I didn't even know half the things Tray was going through. We were all just trying to deal with everything on our own. None of us ever talked about things. Even if our problems seemed small, problems are still problems. How everybody feels still matters.

So I dip my brush back in my paint, and over our faces, I add question marks. It's a reminder. That we should always ask.

Moving Forward

After I finish my painting, I know who I need to call: Kayla. I need to apologize to her.

I lie across my bed and tap my screen for FaceTime. I shift around while it rings, trying to find a comfortable spot for this conversation. After what feels like ages, she answers.

"Heyy Kayla, you look pretty."

She blushes and rolls her eyes. "Thank you." She takes a long pause and says, "Long time no speak."

"How have you been?"

"Uuum sick, remember? Not that you cared."

I pretend to gasp, as if I don't know what she's talking about. Then I immediately regret it. Apologies are awkward, you know? But I just gotta say it before I make things worse.

"About that. I'm so so sorry. I should have called. I don't know what I was thinking. I just needed to take some time to myself."

I pause to wait for her to say something, but she's silent. I think she's pretty angry, and honestly, I don't blame her. She's been trying all this time to get me to let her in, and instead...

"Look," I say, trying to win her back. "Over quarantine, I realized that I wasn't dealing with things the best. I want to apologize for not... talking to you. About any of it. And for not, you know, taking how you felt seriously."

The other end is still silent, but somehow I can feel a

shift, a small one. Or maybe I just hope I do.

"I just was so upset. I just…"

I try to continue but I'm worried I might break down again. I'm not ready for her to see that. Not yet.

"Well," she says, filling my empty space, "how 'bout next time you tell me, instead of ghosting me?" She laughs, clearly trying to stop herself from getting emotional, too.

"Kayla, I promise I'll do right by you this time. I love you. And you're right — we need to talk more. I should have listened."

Kayla stares at me in my soul for what feels like five minutes straight, then takes a deep breath. "Okay," she says. "Over this break, I've had time to think, too. You hurt me, but I can understand. I've seen that you not only ghosted me, you've been away from the world. You haven't been on social media or anything. And I know—" she pauses, like she might not finish her thought. "I know what you must have been going through, not being able to make it to Tray's funeral…"

Her saying his name is like an opening. We both feel it, I think.

"I… should have called you, too," she continues. "I was thinking about you. But you know, you weren't really talking to me." She looks around awkwardly. "I can't imagine… how it must have felt? To have to go through all of that, alone, in your room."

"Yeah," I say. "Honestly? I just kind of lost it."

"So why didn't you call me? At the end of the day, I

am still your girlfriend."

"I know. I realize now it's not healthy to go through it all alone. I feel like I was in one of my darkest moments. I finally had to address it — losing my best friend." It feels good to finally tell someone, to tell her.

"Jiy, I get it. I understand. I guess I can accept your apology." She smiles. "Let's move on." I can still hear the emotion in her voice, but her shoulders have dropped, and she looks like my girl again.

After that we talk for hours. I tell her about all the things I've been feeling during quarantine, and how I can't wait to get out and do something. I tell her how upset I've been about all the holidays we've missed, and family that didn't get to come.

Kayla says, "We been through a lot. We should celebrate! It's our last day of quarantine!"

And that gives me an idea...

Clean Hands

Saturday, January 2, 2021

The next day, I surprise Angel, Dad, and Kayla with a "Redoing New Year's" party to make up for all the time we lost. I invite all the friends, and I even get Uncle Mark to call off work and drive down for the weekend.

I set up balloons, snacks, and a photo booth in the front yard. We gotta be outside for safety but luckily it's not too cold. Our decorations are lit. It looks like it's really New Year's Eve, even though it's actually January 2. The neighbors probably think we're crazy or something.

When everyone gets there, I'm so happy. Seeing everyone's faces again, even six feet apart, makes me feel somewhat whole again. Things are looking so much better. I'm finally back and cool with Kayla. The house is back to normal — no more isolation or breakfast through the door. It feels so good to be able to hug Pops and Angel again. And I even put my man, Tray, right beside me on my lock screen. Now every time I get a notification, I see that picture of me and him playing ball. I carry him with me.

We all put our masks on and crowd around Angel's iPad to watch the ball drop and let off a Roman candle, even though it's the middle of the day. I can't wait to leave 2020 and all of the stress, denial, and secrets behind me. But I won't leave behind what I learned. I'm starting this new year right... even if I am a little late.

COUNCIL OF THE DISTRICT OF COLUMBIA
THE JOHN A. WILSON BUILDING
1350 PENNSYLVANIA AVENUE, N.W.
WASHINGTON, D.C. 20004

JANUARY 4, 2021

DC COUNCIL STATEMENT ON THIS WEEK'S DEMONSTRATIONS IN THE DISTRICT

WASHINGTON, DC — The District of Columbia Council issued the following statement today:

We urge people to avoid the downtown and federal areas where permits for events have been issued for January 5 and 6. In similar recent events, white supremacists and militia groups have created conflict and provoked violence, creating harm for individuals and to our institutions. We urge residents to recognize these are the voices of those who have already lost. Votes have been certified and the demonstrations this week will not change the outcome of this election. There is no gain for all people who desire peace in engaging with those who come here with malicious intent, and doing so only brings great risk.

The peaceful transfer of power following a free and fair election is a cornerstone of our democracy. Any efforts to disenfranchise voters and overturn the will of the electors is nothing short of betraying our very American democracy and should be strongly condemned by all.

The District of Columbia is no stranger to peaceful demonstrations and protecting individuals' rights to exercise their First Amendment. In an unequivocal and unanimous voice, we also condemn hate and the actions witnessed against District residents, faith-based institutions, and the District's core values in the past months — specifically actions to destroy symbols that proclaim that Black Lives Matter. This Council has time and again worked to strengthen our laws and all legal protections against hate. We stand ready to protect our residents.

We recognize that downtown is home to residents and businesses whose rights must be respected and protected as we work to keep all safe, including residents who are currently homeless. We call upon the Mayor's Office, the Metropolitan Police Department (MPD), and coordinating agencies to ensure this is a priority as events go forward this week. Further, we call on MPD and all law enforcement to ensure safety, prevent violence, and to do so with no appearance of preference or disparate treatment.

#

FIRE ON MY DOORSTEP

by Bilal Saleem

Monday, January 4, 2021

New job, new year, new president. It's all in the cards this year.

I quickly finished my breakfast and dumped the plates in the sink, rushing to my desk in time for my first staff meeting. It may have been winter break, but, unfortunately, the grind doesn't stop when college does. I was excited to get to work though, not only to make some spending money, but to spice up my résumé as well.

I grabbed my laptop and ran down the stairs to my room, adjusting my tie to go along with my freshly-cleaned cream shirt. Little would my boss or coworkers know that I was also sporting my favorite pair of Nike sweatpants, one of the perks of only being visible from the chest up on-camera. While I wasn't going to be in an office working face-to-face for the foreseeable future, being able to watch ESPN in the background and wear sweatpants while at work would most definitely be sweet.

It was so wild to be working a job now. Just a year ago, my freshman year was stifled by COVID and since then, it's all been a blur. Now, all of a sudden, I'm employed? Wild.

"Morning everybody," my boss, Jasmine, said. "Nice to virtually see you all."

I wonder if they're all wearing sweatpants too.

"Today we have a new employee joining our staff! Ali, feel free to introduce yourself," Jasmine said.

Oh great, icebreakers. "Hey everyone! Nice to meet you all, my name's Ali. Um, I'm nineteen, I'm a sophomore at the University of Maryland, and I'm really looking forward to working with everybody," I said. "Other than that, I guess I'm into sports, music, and all the other things college kids like me are into."

One by one, I heard introductions of my coworkers. There were only a few employees to get to know, since the company was a budding financial services startup, but that didn't stop my general feeling of elation. I'd always wanted to work in finance, so for a college kid, this was a pretty cool first step.

"What are you looking forward to in the New Year?" one of my new coworkers, Scott, asked.

Damn. How do I tell him, "Dude, I honestly have no idea. I've just been so tired lately. Tired of the pandemic, tired of school, tired of politics, tired of small talk. The list goes on and on. After the election, I think everyone's just hoping for a breath of fresh air, me included. We need some time to decompress and unpack..." But everyone's tired, so I settled for something easy — sports.

"Oh, you know, just hoping that my Terrapins make the Final Four in March. I know it won't happen under our current coach, but a man can dream," I said with a sigh.

When everyone is living the same life, and we're all witnessing history before our eyes, small talk really becomes small. It just feels silly to mention basketball as something to look forward to in 2021, given that there's so much other important shit going on. But, to be honest, when the impending pressure of possible global demise looms in your mind 24/7, sometimes you can't help but escape to something comforting like basketball. Or video games. Or music. Or... anything else.

"Well my alma mater sucks at basketball, so I'll root for the Terps on your behalf! Hopefully I can keep a somewhat accurate bracket this year," Scott said.

"I appreciate that, we'll take any and all support. Go Terps!" I cheered.

Nice, a friend at work already. I'll take it.

My phone lit up. Twenty new messages in the group chat. Wonder what they're talking about this time...

Curtis

yo did y'all mess with Cudi's album?

Hassan

It was alright. I feel like Cudi is so
consistent in general, but there were
a couple of misses on this one.

Blake

I haven't listened yet.

Ashwin

bro it was fire, the production
was unreal and Solo Dolo III
was a godsend, go peep that.

...and the messages go on.

Seeing their names pop up made me miss the squad. I
even missed arguing about all the random stuff we'd talk
about when we were still on campus. I thought about how
it had truly been a minute since I had the opportunity
to connect with new people. Despite having a couple of
in-person classes last semester, I'd had to social distance
and keep the chairs to my left and right empty. When I
had classes online, there was no interaction with other
students, just a bunch of unengaged squares with no
faces watching a shared lecture. Being in a new work
environment gave me the chance to be social, a privilege
that had waned since the onset of the pandemic.

My boss instructed me to shadow Scott, my fellow

basketball fan.

Although he was only a couple years older than me, he knew the industry inside and out, and I could just tell that by shadowing him, I'd learn the skills I needed to be set. He and I popped into a breakout room to talk one-on-one.

"You been surviving all this craziness?" Scott asked. He had a playful aura, but seemed genuinely interested in my answer. That felt rare these days, which made me feel comfortable sharing.

"I don't even know, man. That election? That shit was ridiculous," I said. "Oh, shit, am I allowed to swear?"

Scott laughed, and even through the screen, I could feel his easygoing vibe. Sometimes, you just know that someone lives on the same wavelength as you. Nothing beats that instant feeling of understanding and respect.

"Don't worry, bro. It's all good. Screw the whole system, honestly. I couldn't believe half of what went down these past few years, or how they got away with it."

"No lies there. I just don't know what to even think, you feel me?" I sighed.

"Yeah. We just need to start steering this country in the right direction."

I couldn't help but think, *What is the right direction?* It seemed like everyone had their own idea. I just hoped the truth would set us free 'cause I was tired of being stuck inside. I guess we'd find out, one way or the other. 2021, here we come.

Tuesday, January 5, 2021

Damn, it's cold.

I probably should've brought a jacket, but it didn't go with the fit. Instead, I sacrificed warmth for a burgundy button-down (cuffs rolled-up of course), a pair of black slacks, and some frosty cement-white Jordan 4s. Gotta do what you gotta do, right? My mama's constant nagging to "always bring a coat" lowkey stays backfiring — sometimes I'll leave my coat at home just to get her blood pumping. I mean, I know my naano always would yell at her if she even tried leaving the house without a jacket, so I'm glad I have at least a little more leeway.

The adrenaline of being out in the city with my friends instead of just seeing their names on my phone kept me warm enough though, as we hadn't seen each other in over a month. We'd been friends since freshman year, when we'd all lived in the same hall. Despite us all coming from very different backgrounds, we hit it off, bonding over music, sports, food, and school. We've got Ashwin, known on the basketball court as the South Indian Steph Curry. There's Curtis, who's Black and born and raised in Silver Spring. Can't forget about Hassan, the Punjabi Prince hailing from Philly (which unfortunately makes him a sad 76ers fan). There's Blake, a white boy from Howard County who's in the business school with me. And, of course, there's me, the Pakistani kid from Rockville. We had lots of different perspectives, but generally even more respect. I was hyped to see them in person again.

Despite living so close to DC, I hadn't actually made my way into the city in a brick, mostly due to the pandemic. The Metro had been on limited service, and it's not like 9:30 Club was open for concerts or anything. Regardless, I'd finally made it. We met up on U Street, one of my favorite places to cool it in the city.

"Yo, Ali. What's the move?" Curtis asked.

"Maybe get something to eat? Are y'all with that?" I said.

"Yeah, I'm down, bro. Let's go," Ashwin said.

As we walked along U Street, we couldn't help but notice how desolate the city was — Ben's Chili Bowl without the typical line-out-the-door, and Roaming Rooster with chairs stacked on the tables. Granted, it was freezing out and it was a Tuesday night, but something about the District just felt lonely and empty.

"Man, it's dead out here," Hassan said.

"The 'Rona got everybody on edge — it is what it is. But it does suck," Curtis agreed.

"You all are overreacting. It's peaceful out here," Blake said.

"Lowkey, Blake's right. Nothing like a cold, empty city to make you feel like the main character. Either way, we out here, right? Let's step to DC Noodles. I haven't been in a minute but it's fire," I said.

"Bet, let's go," Curtis said, and they all agreed.

COVID meant that we'd have to eat outside, so it was

a good thing we were going for hot soup and they had heat lamps. During dinner, we did what we normally do. It was like no time had passed at all, honestly, as we sat there chopping it up about sports, music, and whatever else came to mind.

"You're bugging if you think the Giants win their division this year," I said.

"Bruh, we got a better chance than your Ravens," Ashwin sneered.

"There simply ain't no way. Injury-free, we got one of the best rosters in the League. Y'all think Daniel Jones is the future? That actually geeks me," I laughed.

"Bruh, Ashwin, you're actually tripping, the Giants are probably gonna finish last place in their division," Blake chimed in.

"I don't know shit about football, but to me, it sounds like the general consensus is that Ashwin is tripping," Curtis said.

"Man, shut the hell up. The only time Ali puffs up his chest is when he's ragging on my team, but trust me Giants comeback is about to be legendary," Ashwin went on.

"Whatever, bruh. That's all you," I teased.

While we waited for the bill, I checked my phone and saw a headline on Twitter talking about a 'Stop the Steal' rally being planned in DC. It looked like some Trump supporters were getting ready to come to the city from all over and protest the election.

I can't believe they just won't let it go.

"You guys hear about this rally?" I asked.

"What rally?" Ashwin asked.

"Not sure. Apparently, there's some sort of demonstration or some shit. I think they're protesting the election, but who knows," Curtis said.

"To be honest, that election was a bit fishy," Blake said.

Hassan and Curtis looked up from their bowls. I put my phone back in my pocket and looked at them, tension building in the air. It wasn't the first time Blake had said something out-of-pocket, but I always preferred to keep it chill rather than make it a big deal. Ashwin made a sharp exhale.

"You're joking, right?" Ashwin said sternly.

"Nah, you're bugging right now, Blake," Curtis said.

"Stick to football takes, bro," I chirped nervously, patting Blake on the shoulder. That's all I had energy to say.

I was still stuck on how Trump could have a rally for an election he lost anyway. And now this dude Blake was trying to validate him? I swallowed the thought, not wanting to ruin the night. "Let's step."

One of my favorite parks in DC, Malcolm X Park (known by the National Park Service as Meridian Hill Park), was just a few minutes away. When I was growing up, my family and I would go there on Sundays to watch the drum circle. I always loved how diverse and vibrant it was, with people from all races and backgrounds, people unified in their differences, celebrating along to a single beat. I thought it'd be a good place to chop it up a bit more before we all headed home.

As we walked towards the park, I noticed "For Lease" signs and doors boarded up in plywood. It was disheartening to see the city I loved so deeply struggle and shudder as COVID kept landing blow after blow. Mom-and-Pop shops that had been around since I was young, corner stores where you could grab a quick bite, all breathing their last breaths out into the cold and unsympathetic asphalt.

But then we passed 14th Street and saw racks of electric scooters, new condominiums that would sell for millions, and a Lululemon. The aura that I felt walking by these flashy new developments was even colder than the blocks behind us. What was once a historically Black part of the city, teeming with a unique local culture and vibrance, was now becoming hollow.

As we got to the park, we saw a group of kids running around with a box of leftover firecrackers from New Years, tossing them at each other like crab apples. We could hear nonstop shouts of joy and laughter, with the occasional screech of pain. It was such a little thing, a group of friends creating excitement and delight, and it made us stop wallowing in despair and just take in the night. We sat down by the Joan of Arc statue overlooking the lights of the city. The massive fountain that typically flowed down the hill below us wasn't running, but it still felt like a powerful place. My parents used to tell me this was where people like Duke Ellington, Thurgood Marshall,

Angela Davis, and even Malcolm X himself used to gather. I was in awe of the ways they'd all spoken truth to power. I looked at my friends living in the joy of the moment despite the wilderness of this past year and thought about what it would feel like for us to make that kind of impact on the world. That was one of the things I liked most about coming into DC — you felt like you were right in the middle of something, like you were a part of history.

Little did I know how true that would feel the very next day.

Wednesday, January 6, 2021

"Oh my. Ali, you have to see this."

I looked up from my laptop and saw Mama, shocked, staring at the TV.

"What the hell?" I gasped. My jaw doesn't usually drop like a character from the Looney Tunes, but witnessing an attack on the Capitol isn't something you see every afternoon. Confederate flags and M.A.G.A. memorabilia were everywhere, and there was a large mob of Trump supporters attempting to *break into the Capitol Building* and *overturn the election.* Such a ludicrous statement is something that I thought I'd only hear in a dystopian movie where half of humankind had become zombies and the sky was falling, but, as Childish Gambino said, *This Is America.*

"Baba just called me from the grocery store, telling me to turn on the news. These rioters are convinced the election was a fraud," Mama said.

"This is way more than a riot. This is, like, terrorism," I said.

"Yep, and this guy on the news is calling it a protest."

"I mean, I'm not really surprised. They've been saying the election has been 'fake' or 'falsified' for a hot minute anyway. The real question is, where the hell are the police?"

"I don't know, maybe they're waiting for orders," Mama sighed.

I doubted that.

My younger brother Zain, Mama, and I sat in awe as we watched the attackers, who were covered in dust and army surplus store apparel, break down the doors to the Capitol and start rummaging around inside. C-SPAN footage was hitting Twitter faster than it was hitting our TV, so with each pull-down and refresh on my feed, we were stunned: videos of men in camouflage screaming for the head of Nancy Pelosi, pictures of Confederate flags draped over chairs in the Senate chambers, and one officer who was going viral for trying to lead the mob away.

"What's that guy doing?" Zain asked.

"The cop? It looks like he was trying to stop the terrorists from getting into an important area. Maybe the Senate chambers?" I responded.

"Yeah, maybe. So brave of him to stand up to them," Mama said.

As the coverage continued, the living room atmosphere just got more and more sullen. I don't even remember 9/11 (I was only six months old then), but I definitely experienced the ignorance and hate that this country carried afterwards for folks who were Muslim, or who even "looked" Muslim. For years, I'd come across little microaggressions or, well, full-on insults. "Go back to yer' country" or "shut up, terrorist" were some of the more common ones. Not gonna lie, it hurt. But I learned to blend in. Swallow my tongue. Now, for the first time, I was seeing that same type of ignorance and hate materialize into an entire movement. A movement taking

place not fifteen miles from *my* house. I felt scared and
confused. And most of all, I was pissed.

There was tension and resentment in the air. And it
wasn't because of what these rioters were doing. It was the
lack of consequences.

"If they looked like us they'd be dead already," Zain
spoke up.

"Don't say that, who knows what would have happened,"
Mama said sternly.

"Come on, Mama. You know that if this crowd was
anything but predominantly white, but *especially* if they
were Black or brown, they'd have called in the National
Guard already, or activated the sleeper turrets that they
probably have concealed in each pillar. There'd be no
hesitation to call them terrorists like these news channels
are clearly refraining from doing," I said.

I was interrupted by a phone call from Scott.

"Hey, Ali. I assume you saw the news?" Scott started.

"Unfortunately, I have it on right now. I've never seen
anything like this. Terrifying stuff," I sighed.

"Yeah, well, what can you do?" he chuckled.

He sounded unbothered. Like we weren't watching the
same thing.

"I mean, yeah, it's actually unbelievable. I had heard
some buzz on Twitter about a demonstration of sorts, but I
didn't think there'd be a full-on coup today," I said uneasily.

"I don't know, man. But hey, let's see how it turns out.
The markets are definitely going to be a mess tomorrow.

Anyway, just calling to let you know that Jasmine's giving everybody the rest of the day off. And oh yeah, can you make sure you get your onboarding documents in by Friday? Jasmine keeps pushing me about them," he said.

"Uh... sure, I guess," I responded.

What the hell was that? The Capitol is burning but he's asking me about paperwork?

Not what I expected, but after today, or even this past year, my expectations were on the floor. I turned to see Mama still on the couch, with her classic furrowed brow, angrily asking questions.

"What do they possibly think can even happen from this?" Mama said in disgust.

"Well, clearly they think they can overturn the election. Obviously, it won't happen, though," Zain said.

"God, I hope not," Mama said.

We sat in silence, eyes glued to the TV. So much was happening that my brain went static from the sensory overload.

"Look," Mama said. "As much as I'd like to see this mob get cleared out the way we would be if it were us, it doesn't change the fact that there are two Americas. And they're being pitted against each other, and they won't communicate. Just wait. The story of this day is going to be told very differently in different homes in the coming days."

"How can you be so calm about this?" I asked.

"These are the same people who tried to stop people like us from coming to the United States. The people who supported a full-on Muslim ban. How are you supposed to communicate with someone like that?"

"I don't know how. But they're bringing the fire to our doorstep, and we can either respond with water or gasoline. What's the smarter move to make?"

I didn't have an answer. I looked at my phone to see if my friends had texted, but for the first time during the pandemic, the group chat was dead silent. None of us had any answers today, I guess.

Fatal Insurrection at US Capitol Leaves DC Under Curfew, Public Emergency

January 6, 2021

Trump supporters break into the Capitol, Wednesday, Jan. 6 2021.

Tyler Merbler

Thursday, January 7, 2021

I hopped into the work Zoom meeting the next morning expecting people to be talking about what went down at the Capitol, but to my surprise, everyone seemed to be carrying on business-as-usual. They were actually talking about Elon Musk's net worth and how he'd overtaken Jeff Bezos' spot as the "richest man in the world."

"The Tesla Man did it! 185 billion. Who would've thought?" Scott said.

"Surely Bezos is wiping his tears away with blue hundreds as we speak," some guy named Wyatt said.

Jasmine chimed in, "You both are ridiculous. But let's make a note to add Tesla stock to our call list… Anyway, wild day yesterday, folks. Hope you enjoyed your brief time off, because we have a lot to talk about this morning. Let's go over our agenda for the day."

Damn. I thought at least as the boss she'd say something about, like, unprecedented attacks on democracy or something, but it's radio silence out here.

She went on about our options strategies for the coming weeks, how our client portfolios were faring, and whether we wanted to incorporate a bearish or bullish strategy on some new IPOs. It was all about charts, projections, and growth, but nothing about the attack or the National Guard being called in.

Like how often does this shit happen? Say something!

I started getting frustrated, pressure building on my

shoulders. I turned my camera off for a second to try and cool off and picked up my phone to send a text to Scott.

Ali

hey man, are we really not gonna talk about yesterday?

Scott

idk dude, what's the point?

Ali

weren't you talking about how we need to screw the whole system? wouldn't talking about it be more helpful than sweeping it under the rug?

Scott

this country already has so much stuff under the rug

So what, you just wanna smile and wave? Nothing sucked more than feeling like someone who understood or respected you wasn't hearing you at all. I thought about the first day at work and how comfortable I felt thinking I had him on my side. Like he was someone I could look up to, who could show me the ropes. I knew finance was a cutthroat industry with little room for feelings, especially about politics, but did that mean that I had to swallow my voice forever? Even when the country was on fire? That was definitely not the impact I wanted to have. *This dude really isn't who I thought he was.*

I let out a frustrated grunt and I decided to text the squad and see what they thought about the whole situation. They'd have my back, and I trusted them to hear me out.

Ali

> yo, corporate ppl are hella cold

Ashwin

> fr? what happened?

Ali

> i joined the zoom meeting, thinking we'd talk about the capitol yesterday, but they were deadass talking about elon musk and jeff bezos

Hassan

> Damn, that's wack. Like you guys know I'm not super political but we just witnessed history yesterday, you'd think they'd be talking about it

Ali

right? i texted one of my coworkers who i thought i was cool with asking him if we were gonna talk about it and he just brushed it off. asked me "what's the point" like attacks on the capitol are chill

Curtis

that's def not okay bruh

Blake

I get that you're frustrated, but I mean, what is the point though? Like, protests happen all the time. It seems like ppl are only pissed because it happened on the right. Just what I've noticed tho.

Protest? That was a terrorist attack. I stared at Blake's comment, wanting to give him the benefit of the doubt. We'd been friends for a while now. It's not like we talked about politics a lot, but… *come on, dude, you can't be that ignorant.*

Curtis

> bro, it was NOT a protest. bringing
> a guillotine to the capitol and then
> breaking in to overturn an election?
> that's not just any old protest, it's
> domestic terrorism.

Hassan

> True but I mean there's all types of
> protests, we can just leave it at that.

At this point, my camera had been off for a few
minutes so that my coworkers couldn't see me, and I could
feel my face turning red. I knew Blake was white and had
a different experience in this country than, well, all of
us, but even still he couldn't act like "it's all good" or like
"these things happen." I mean, if domestic terrorism wasn't
something we condemned, then where did we draw the
line? I was all for respecting other perspectives, especially
when it led to engaging conversation, but this was making
my stomach hurt. It felt like it was always up to people of
color to respect the perspectives that hurt them. His name
popped up on my screen again. *Ugh.*

Blake

> Well if ur gonna call yesterday
> a terrorist attack, then what
> about during BLM when people
> were setting buildings on fire?
> I mean I guess I'm not really
> seeing the difference

Curtis

> there's a big difference...

Ashwin

> nah blake, the caucasity
> is glaring rn

Was Blake really like this? Had he been thinking these things all along?

Hassan

> Come on, guys. He's just trying
> to learn

Ashwin

> we go to a big, diverse, state
> school. he could've learned
> already if he really wanted to

Blake

> That's pretty rude to say. There was
> more damage done during BLM than
> whatever happened yesterday. All I'm
> saying is terrorists don't run around
> with American flags.

Ashwin

> what flags do terrorists run
> around with then?

My hand formed a fist on the desk, anticipating his response.

Curtis

> yea i don't have the energy to explain
> how wrong you are rn

Curtis left the conversation.

Blake

> Damn I didn't think it was that
> serious. What's his problem?

Even if he didn't usually say much, Curtis was a kind of anchor for our group, so getting him to the point where he left the chat was... *Sheesh.* He was right though — it shouldn't be our job to always put people in their place. People who never did their due diligence to learn how the world worked for people other than them. It was exhausting and unfair to us. And finally, I was fed up.

Ali

> if you can't comprehend the fact that BLM is a movement designed to seek justice and the terrorist attack yesterday was a last-ditch attempt by a failing president to try and undermine our democracy, then idk what else to say.

> i'm tired of people acting like "it is what it is" and i'm tired of you, right now, dismissing literal terrorism because we have the "freedom to do whatever we want"

> your ignorance is one of the reasons America is falling apart.

There. I said it. No more blending in. No more holding back. I waited for what felt like an eternity for Blake to respond. Then finally:

Blake

America's not perfect bro.
If u don't like it, then leave.

I sat there, phone-in-hand, seeing red. I stayed that
way for at least two minutes before I was able to respond.
I thought about all the times I'd heard some rendition
of this phrase. How quickly it made me feel alienated,
anxious, and scared. As if I didn't belong in the country I
called home. And now, it hit me even harder when it came
from someone who I thought was my friend, from the
group that, especially over the last year, had become a kind
of home, too.

He'd finally gone too far. The sad truth was that you
didn't have to try to be racist to say something racist.
And one of my friends had just said something racist. I
couldn't keep myself from putting gasoline on this fire.
Microaggressions left and right, in school, in the office, in
my hometown, and now here. *I should've drawn the line a
long time ago, but I was definitely drawing it now.*

Ali

why don't u go back to europe,
colonizer? i was born here, my
parents were born here, idk who
the hell you think you are

Blake

> Dude, relax. I didn't mean for it to sound like that, but that doesn't give you the right to call me a colonizer.

Hassan

> Broooo, chill, Ali. idk if he knows what he's saying.

Ashwin

> saying "then leave" even if it's a joke is one of the most deep-rooted racist things someone can say in our country. one of the og microaggressions. blake you're so out of pocket it's unreal

I had been trying, at least a little bit, to check my temper and let shit slide to keep this group together, but this was the final straw.

Ali

> go to hell, blake

Ali left the conversation.

Friday, January 8, 2021

I logged off early from work the next day, figuring nobody would need me after 3:00 p.m. on a Friday anyway. I needed to get out of the house.

"Mama, I'm gonna take the car, is that cool?" I asked. I went into the kitchen to grab a quick glass of water before heading out. Mama was sitting at the table on her laptop, and I moved in a hurry to avoid making eye contact.

"Yeah, no problem. Just drive safe and don't come back too late," she replied.

I don't know how she even noticed, but Mama's sixth sense kicked in and she could tell something was off.

"Hey, are you good?" she asked.

"Yeah, I'm alright. Just got into it with some friends yesterday. But it's all good, don't really wanna talk about it. I just need some space from them."

"Yikes, with your *friends?* That's tough. Do you think you'll be able to sort it out?"

I could still feel the rage from Blake's words. *If you don't like it, then leave.*

"I don't know. I don't think so."

"Oh man, I'm sorry."

"Yeah. It sucks."

"It definitely does. But I'm here for you. It'll be alright."

"Yeah. Thanks, Mama." I said before giving her a hug.

She kissed my forehead before playfully hitting my shoulder, adding:

"Also, take your freaking coat."

Bruh. Who needs a coat in the car? Whatever.

I reluctantly grabbed my jacket and made a break for the door.

I was still blown after everything that went down yesterday, and figured that some good music and a scenic drive might calm my psyche. If nothing else got my mind right, my Spotify library surely could. *Dawn FM* by the Weeknd would be the perfect soundtrack to decompress.

I had assumed that I-495 was going to be gridlocked like usual, but it was actually smooth sailing for the most part. I pulled off the Beltway onto GW Parkway and took a deep breath. Despite the leisurely drive, I noticed that my knuckles were white from gripping the steering wheel too hard.

White knuckles. White privilege. Sigh.

I shook my head. What Blake had said yesterday made me question who I could trust. It wasn't just the fact that he was completely tone-deaf, it was that he felt justified in what he said. And Scott, too. Clearly I read him wrong. How could he have been so unbothered? It's like neither of them understood what it felt like to be on the wrong side of justice. Or like they even cared enough to empathize.

As I drove closer to DC along the Potomac, the Gothic gray spires of Georgetown University came into view, and then the Washington Monument, peeking out in the distance. Despite the lack of leaves on the trees, the scenes on GW Parkway were beautiful. But the beauty was tempered by the reminders of the week's events — every single exit had at least one or two squad cars posted on the ramp, with their lights on and everything. It was eerie in a way. You couldn't help feeling like something terrible had happened. Or like something terrible was still happening.

What was becoming increasingly clear, this year more than ever, was that there were a lot of competing truths out there. And they didn't all line up. There was Curtis', Ashwin's, Hassan's, and as much as it pained me to admit it, even Scott's and Blake's. My truth wasn't the only one.

I was trying to unpack all the different pieces of my identity, and it was not easy. As a young, brown, Muslim, American, Pakistani, cisgender male, there was just so much to think about. And it was exhausting, man. There were ways that my life had led me to really get fired up about hate and prejudice and injustice, because I had experienced it. I knew what it was like to feel *othered*. But I was so fortunate, too — I had a stable family, I was in college, I was even blessed with a job. These were all parts of my own privilege. So, where did I fit in? How should I carry myself? When did my privilege contribute to my own ignorance, and when did it allow me to actually have an impact? It was hard to untangle all of this. And especially since the world started falling apart, it was easy to feel like I was all alone in it.

I took the exit for I-66 towards Roosevelt Bridge, crossing over the Potomac, continuing to mull over these questions. There had been too many times that

I'd kept my own feelings inside, not saying what I really meant in order to keep the peace. And that meant people didn't really know who I was. Maybe if I had done more speaking my truths than swallowing them, I wouldn't be feeling all resentful about losing a friend, or losing faith in people overall.

I'd wanted to drive past the monuments along the National Mall, but it was totally blocked off with barricades and police lights everywhere. I heard they'd fenced off the whole area but could barely believe it until I saw it myself. So I turned up through GW's campus instead, driving uptown, unsure of where I was going but feeling like maybe I was heading in the right direction. I turned on L Street, then made a left onto 16th. As I went further and further up, I realized that I was on the same route toward Malcolm X Park that I had taken on Tuesday. It had only been three days since I was there, and yet, with all the shit that went down, it felt like forever.

When I got to the top of the hill, by the entrance, I decided to park. I got out of my car and slowly made my way towards the overlook. My footsteps crunched the half-frozen grass. The sun was out, and despite the cold, the neighborhood kids were zooming around on their bikes. Among them, there was a group of boys joking and pushing each other, which made me remember those times I'd spent afternoons doing the same.

In some ways, it felt like a regular Friday afternoon. And in others, it felt historic. Someday my kids would be reading about this week, this whole past year, in their textbooks, and I'd be telling them what it was like, living through this wild time in DC. What would I say? Would this be a turning point for our country? Would it be a turning point for me?

It was hard to feel optimistic after the last few days, and yet, something about the warmth of the sun, and the neighborhood kids seizing the day, and the courage of the people who had stood *in this very spot...* it made me feel like change was possible. I breathed in the moment along with the brisk winter air. I knew I wasn't alone in my flaws, and I hoped I wasn't alone in wanting to be better. Mostly I hoped that someday we could all come to terms with what it meant to hold different truths, reconciling both the beauty and the lessons in our differences, and celebrate along to a single beat.

ACKNOWLEDGMENTS

This book would not be possible without the hard work and dedication of ten young people committed to the dream of this book: Deyssy, T'Asia, Iman, Camal, Tatiana, Saylenis, Darne'Sha, Joseph, Najae, and Bilal. We are grateful for their courage, their vision, and their willingness to speak their truths.

Thank you to acclaimed author and all-around stellar human being, Candice Iloh, for writing the foreword to this book, and for holding our authors' work close to their heart. We're grateful for their affirmation and endorsement of these important voices.

We always feel gratitude for our dedicated team at Shout Mouse Press, which includes a wide range of teaching artists, writers, editors, designers, and publishing professionals. We could not fully enact the mission of this project without the hard work of our Story Coaches — Drew Anderson, Faith Campbell, Alexa Patrick, Tatiana Figueroa Ramirez, and Barrett Smith — who met weekly to support each author as they wrote their stories. We are grateful for their commitment to centering youth voices and problem-solving through a year of imagining, drafting, and revising. We thank illustrators Sade Adeshida, Rae Flores, Vivian Jones, Courtney Williams Skinner, and Alexis Williams for their tremendous portraits, and for meeting individually with each author to capture the essence of their protagonists. Thank you for bringing their characters to life! We are always thankful for designer Gigi Mascareñas, who worked tirelessly to design the striking cover, create compelling visual elements, and otherwise ensure that our writers' work is presented professionally and with great attention and care. And finally, thanks are due to those working behind the scenes: Programs Director Alexa Patrick thoughtfully led program design and individual revision sessions; Publishing Manager Dave Ring and Operations Manager Barrett Smith provided essential editorial and design support; and Executive Director Kathy Crutcher edited these stories in a way that strives to honor these young people and their mission.

In closing, we are grateful for the generous financial support from both individuals and institutions that make our work possible, including the DC Commission on Arts and Humanities. We appreciate your investment in our work, and most importantly, in the young people whose voices sing from these pages.

SOURCES

We took our role as historical fiction writers seriously, rooting all fictionalized original stories within accurate historical context. This meant fact-checking all stories for accuracy, placing them within a chronology and geography of real-world events. We referred to actual newspaper headlines and other media coverage to inform and complement our stories; all photographs are either original to the Shout Mouse team or used with permission. Our complete list of citations follows. We encourage you to follow the links and read these first drafts of history.

SPRING
The Storm, the Rainbow, and Valentina

15   *COVID map graphic*
            Kopecki, Dawn, et al. "US Coronavirus Death Toll Rises to 9,
                Mortality Rate of COVID-19 Rises." *CNBC*, 4 Mar. 2020,
                www.cnbc.com/2020/03/03/coronavirus-latest-updates-
                outbreak.html. Accessed 18 Dec. 2022.

15   *Christ Episcopal Church — Georgetown image*
            Graf, Heather (ABC7). "Christ Church Georgetown's Father
                Tim Cole, a COVID-19 Survivor, Shares Easter Message."
                WJLA, 10 Apr. 2020, wjla.com/news/local/christ-church-
                georgetowns-father-tim-cole-a-covid-19-survivor-shares-
                easter-message. Accessed 18 Dec. 2022.

15   *"District of Columbia announces its..." headline*
            Custis, Aimee. "A Timeline of the D.C. Region's COVID-19
                Pandemic." *D.C. Policy Center*, 24 Mar. 2020, www.
                dcpolicycenter.org/publications/covid-19-timeline.
                Accessed 10 Jan. 2023.

20   *Headlines*
Custis, Aimee. "A Timeline of the D.C. Region's COVID-19 Pandemic." *D.C. Policy Center*, 24 Mar. 2020, www.dcpolicycenter.org/publications/covid-19-timeline. Accessed 10 Jan. 2023.

20   *Phone background image of DC cherry blossoms*
Juarez, Bryants. "Cherry Blossom in Washington D.C." *Pexels*, 3 Apr. 2022, www.pexels.com/photo/cherry-blossom-in-washington-d-c-11625770.

29   *Homemade mask photo*
Dao, Sarah. "Blue Handled Scissors beside Gray and White Towel Photo." *Unsplash*, 11 Apr. 2020, unsplash.com/photos/yUJCffIMR0A.

29   *TikTok trend photo*
Smith, Barrett. Whipped coffee TikTok trend. 9 Apr. 2020.

29   *_faithc profile photo*
Roseclay, Dominika. "Homemade Face Masks near Leaves during COVID 19 Pandemic." *Pexels*, 19 Aug. 2020, www.pexels.com/photo/homemade-face-masks-near-leaves-during-covid-19-pandemic-4289041.

29   *ba.r_r.ett profile photo*
Smith, Barrett. Porch alligator statue covered in snow. 21 Dec. 2020.

SUMMER

Born in Black

112   *"US Coronavirus death toll reaches…" headline*
@Reuters (Reuters). "U.S. coronavirus death toll reaches 100,000 as states reopen." *Twitter*, 27 May 2020, twitter.com/Reuters/status/1265745841618391041.

112   *"Chaotic scene in Minneapolis after…" headline*
Bailey, Holly, et al. "Chaotic Scene in Minneapolis after Second Night of Protests over Death of George Floyd." *The Washington Post*, 28 May 2020, www.washingtonpost.com/nation/2020/05/27/george-floyd-minneapolis-reaction.

Accessed 10 Jan. 2023.

112   *"Demonstrators in DC Gather to..." headline*

Barthel, Margaret, and Christian Zapata. "Demonstrators in D.C. Gather to Protest Death of George Floyd." *DCist*, 29 May 2020, dcist.com/story/20/05/29/crowd-swells-at-14th-u-in-protest-of-george-floyd-killing. Accessed 10 Jan. 2023.

112   *Phone background image*

Flo Dnd. "Photo of Bokeh." *Pexels*, 15 Apr. 2019, www.pexels.com/photo/photo-of-bokeh-2122326.

130   *BLM protest photo*

Kunii, Koshu. "Black Lives Matter Protest in DC, 6/1/2020." *Unsplash*, 1 June 2020, unsplash.com/photos/ILpe0MpOYww. Accessed 4 Jan. 2023.

130–   *Headline, Trump photo caption, and article excerpt*
131   Rucker, Philip, et al. "Trump Mobilizes Military, Threatens to Use Troops to Quell Protests across U.S." *The Washington Post*, 1 June 2020, www.washingtonpost.com/politics/trump-mobilizes-military-threatens-to-use-troops-to-quell-protests-across-us/2020/06/01/10212832-a416-11ea-bb20-ebf0921f3bbd_story.html. Accessed 19 Dec. 2022.

131   *Trump holds bible photo (Creative Commons Attribution License)*

Craighead, Shealah (The White House). "President Trump Visits St. John's Episcopal Church." *Flickr*, 1 June 2020, www.flickr.com/photos/whitehouse45/49963649028. Accessed 19 Dec. 2022.

140   *BLM statue photo*

Crutcher, Kathy. BLM spray-painted on statue. 7 June 2020.

140   *sci.fi-dave profile photo*

Crutcher, Kathy. Black Trans Lives Matter sign. 7 Nov. 2020.

141   *BLM posters photo*

Crutcher, Kathy. Black Lives Matter Plaza fence posters. 7 June 2020.

141   *"This fence is representing that..." caption*

"Here's What Protesters Have Been Saying for the Past Two Weeks." *DCist*, 12 June 2020, dcist.com/story/20/06/12/

heres-what-protesters-have-been-saying-for-the-past-two-
weeks. Accessed 18 Dec. 2022.

142   *"DC Paints Street, Designates it..." headline*
"D.C. Paints Street, Designates It 'Black Lives Matter Plaza'."
NBC4 Washington, 5 June 2020, www.nbcwashington.com/
news/national-international/d-c-paints-street-designates-it-
black-lives-matter-plaza/2324119. Accessed 10 Jan. 2023.

142–   *BLM Plaza photo*
143   Apple Maps. Satellite view of Black Lives Matter Plaza in
Washington, DC. Accessed 18 Dec. 2022.

144   *BLM protest photo*
Tchompalov, Vlad. "June 6, 2020 Protest outside the White House,
Washington DC." *Unsplash*, 7 June 2020, unsplash.com/
photos/eVVrlfbYCzw. Accessed 4 Jan. 2023.

144–   *Headline and article excerpt*
145   Turner, Tyrone (WAMU), and Mary Tyler March. "In Photos:
Looking Back on 12 Days of Protests in D.C." *NPR*, 11 June
2020, www.npr.org/local/305/2020/06/11/874865584/in-
photos-looking-back-on-12-days-of-protests-in-d-c.
Accessed 18 Dec. 2022.

145   *BLM protest photo*
Banks, Clay. "Woman Holds up a Sign at the Black Lives Matter
Protest in Washington DC 6/6/2020." *Unsplash*, 8 June 2020,
unsplash.com/photos/OvGIFsexb-8. Accessed 4 Jan. 2023.

A Little King Is on the Rise

163   *BLM mural photo 1*
Crutcher, Kathy. Black Lives Matter mural of outlined people
protesting with quotes and names. 15 Aug. 2020.

163   *BLM mural photo 2*
Crutcher, Kathy. RIP George Floyd, We Demand Justice mural art
by @uncle_wiink. 2 Aug. 2020.

163   *BLM signage photo 3*
Mascareñas, Gigi. Large Black Lives Matter building signage.
27 June 2020.

163   *BLM mural photo 4*
Crutcher, Kathy. Enough is Enough, Black Lives Matter mural.
2 July 2020.

163   *"I have a young nephew…" and "There's nowhere else for me…" quotes*
"Here's What Protesters Have Been Saying for the Past Two
Weeks." *DCist*, 12 June 2020, dcist.com/story/20/06/12/
heres-what-protesters-have-been-saying-for-the-past-two-
weeks. Accessed 18 Dec. 2022.

FALL
Damaged

187   *Mourning candle photo*
Bronzini, Eva. "Burning Candle on a Candle Stand." *Pexels*, 3 Nov.
2020, www.pexels.com/photo/burning-candle-on-a-candle-
stand-5777247.

Democracy How?

233   *"Americans share what it means…" headline*
Kulkarni, Shefali S., and Eliza Goren. "Americans Share What It
Means to Vote in the 2020 Election." *The Washington Post*,
3 Nov. 2020, www.washingtonpost.com/politics/2020/11/03/
voters-election-reaction. Accessed 23 Dec. 2022.

233   *"Trump falsely asserts election fraud…" headline*
Itkowitz, Colby, et al. "Trump Falsely Asserts Election Fraud,
Claims a Victory." *The Washington Post*, 4 Nov. 2020,
www.washingtonpost.com/elections/2020/11/03/trump-
biden-election-live-updates. Accessed 23 Dec. 2022.

233   *"Biden renews call for patience…" headline*
Viser, Matt, and Toluse Olorunnipa. "Biden Renews Call for
Patience as Trump Assails Vote-Counting Process." *The*

Washington Post, 5 Nov. 2020, www.washingtonpost.com/
politics/biden-trump-election/2020/11/05/1dd15c6c-1f82-
11eb-ba21-f2f001f0554b_story.html. Accessed 23 Dec. 2022.

233   *"Cautious hope and celebration mark…" headline*
Lang, Marissa J. "Cautious Hope and Celebration Mark Rallies
near White House as Battleground Votes Are Counted." *The
Washington Post*, 6 Nov. 2020, www.washingtonpost.com/
local/white-house-rallies-election/2020/11/06/f88d1052-202d-
11eb-b532-05c751cd5dc2_story.html. Accessed 23 Dec. 2022.

233   *Phone background image of Lagos, Nigeria*
FPD Images. "Body of Water under Gloomy Sky." *Pexels*, 30 Apr.
2021, www.pexels.com/photo/body-of-water-under-gloomy-
sky-7596561.

234–   *Photos*
235   Crutcher, Kathy. Photos from Black Lives Matter Plaza in
Washington, DC after election results were announced.
7 Nov. 2020.

235   *tati-the-kitti profile photo*
Pixabay. "Low Angle Shot of a Tabby Cat." *Pexels*, 8 Oct. 2017,
www.pexels.com/photo/low-angle-shot-of-a-tabby-
cat-208984.

235   *drew202 profile photo*
Crutcher, Kathy. Stylized DC flag art from protest poster.
7 June 2020.

WINTER
The Things We Do Not Speak

249   *COVID graphic*
Centers for Disease Control and Prevention. COVID-19 incubation
timeline graphic. *WFLA*, 24 Nov. 2020, www.wfla.com/
community/health/coronavirus/heres-why-its-crucial-to-
quarantine-for-14-days-after-covid-19-exposure. Accessed
18 Dec. 2022.

255   *Christmas ornament photo*
          Crutcher, Kathy. Christmas ornament of 2020 as dumpster fire.
                  28 Nov. 2020.

272–   *DC Council Statement*
273   Council of the District of Columbia. "DC Council Statement on
                  This Week's Demonstrations in the District." 4 Jan. 2021,
                  www.brianneknadeau.com/sites/default/files/2021-01/
                  councilstatementondemonstrations.pdf. Accessed 27 Oct. 2022.

Fire on My Doorstep

291   *"Fatal Insurrection at US Capitol..." headline*
          Grablick, Colleen, et al. "A Fatal Insurrection at the U.S. Capitol
                  Leaves D.C. under Curfew, Public Emergency." *DCist*,
                  6 Jan. 2021, dcist.com/story/21/01/06/dc-trump-election-
                  protest. Accessed 23 Dec. 2022.

291   *January 6 insurrection photo (Creative Commons Attribution License)*
          Merbler, Tyler. "Selfie." *Flickr*, 6 Jan. 2021, www.flickr.com/
                  photos/37527185@N05/50821579347. Accessed 4 Jan. 2023.

ABOUT THE AUTHORS

My name is **T'Asia Bates** (she/her). I was 18 when I wrote my story, "Not What I Signed Up For." This is the second book that I've published with Shout Mouse Press. My first book was *The Day Tajon Got Shot* (2017). I am a graduate of Benjamin Banneker High School and am currently working and trying to reinvent my clothing business. When I am older, I would like to be in the art field, working in fashion, painting, drawing, and modeling.

For me, 2020 was stressful because I was trying to juggle both personal and school struggles. That said, I would draw and make up art projects to keep me busy. I want readers to learn from this book that when things get hard, you can still persevere and find things that make you happy so that you can keep pushing.

My name is **Joseph Chuku** (he/him). When I wrote my story, "Democracy How?," I was a senior in high school. I'm currently

a freshman at Lewis & Clark College. This is my second book with Shout Mouse, as I also helped write the children's book *Shayla's Shutdown Solution* (2020). At this moment in my life, I am trying to find a balance. I have not yet, but I will let you know when I do! In the future, I plan to go to grad school and study medicine in hopes of becoming a radiology oncologist.

For me, 2020 was difficult because I had to rely on myself more than I ever had to before. However, my hope of seeing people again helped me get through the year. I want readers of this book to know that you are never alone.

My name is **Iman Ilias** (she/her). I was 18 years old when I wrote my story, "A Ramadan to Remember." This is my second book with Shout Mouse, as I am also an author of *I Am the Night Sky* (2019). I am currently a freshman at the University of Pennsylvania, studying International Relations and exploring the great Philly food scene. After I graduate, I would love to be a diplomat living in DC and working at the State Department.

For me, 2020 was surprisingly comforting, as I was able to make some lasting memories in my childhood home before moving away for college. Taking walks through my neighborhood every afternoon with my mom and brother made quarantine feel much less stifling. I hope that readers are able to see that the events of 2020 impacted people in all different ways, and that their experiences are shared by others. Even though the pandemic felt isolating for so many, we hope this book makes readers realize that we all went through this tumultuous period together, and that they have people who understand what they went through.

My name is **Deyssy Mosso** (she/her). When I wrote my story, "The Storm, the Rainbow, and Valentina," I was a junior at the  University of the District of Columbia. I am majoring in Social Work and expect to graduate in May 2023. I have already published two other books with Shout Mouse Press: *Voces Sin Fronteras* (2018), and *Perla's Magical Goodbye / El adiós mágico de Perla* (2021). When I am not writing or in classes, I am interning at So Others Might Eat (SOME), working at a local restaurant, or painting! Once I graduate from UDC, I would like to attend law school and enter a full-time job where I can keep helping vulnerable communities.

For me 2020 was a challenge. I learned too much about "life" and how hard and unexpected things can change our lives in one second. But I was also able to reflect and learn: I took more time for myself, I called my mom and my siblings more, and I even improved my writing skills by writing stories. I want to let my readers know that no matter how hard or difficult times can be, there is always a light of hope encouraging you to not give up. As human beings, we are fighters.

My name is **Saylenis Palmore** (she/her). I was 21 years old when I wrote my story, "Damaged." This is the second book that I have published with Shout Mouse Press. I am also one of the authors of *Voces Sin Fronteras* (2018). I am currently a senior at the University of the District of Columbia. Though I am still figuring out what I would like to do when I graduate, I know I would enjoy working for an organization that helps kids around the world.

For me, 2020 was a year of learning and mental growth. Focusing on my school work helped me get through it. I hope that those who read my story learn that we are responsible for our own futures and that it's never too late to start fresh.

My name is **Najae Purvis** (she/her). I was 19 when I started writing my story, "The Things We Do Not Speak." This will be my second book with Shout Mouse Press. I am also one of the authors of *The Day Tajon Got Shot* (2017). I am currently a freshman in college studying engineering and am working on getting business registrations for multiple ventures. I plan on being a licensed architect, realtor, and entrepreneur. In my free time, I like to do creative projects like art, fashion, and design.

For me, 2020 was hard because my life took a huge turn. Everything changed — my lifestyle, friendships, and more. To get through it, I would write poetry, cook, listen to music, reflect, and practice self-care more often. I hope that when people read this book they are fascinated by the different insights and perspectives. I hope that young adults and teens are able to connect with the book and realize that they are not alone. Although their story may not be the exact same, this pandemic all cost us something.

 My name is **Tatiana Robinson** (she/her). I was born and raised in Southeast, DC. I wrote my story, "A Little King Is on the Rise," when I was 20 years old. This is my second book with Shout Mouse Press, as I am also a co-author of *The Ballou We Know* (2019). I am currently a junior at the University of Miami and am a triple major in Interactive Media, Broadcast Journalism, and Communication Studies: Public Advocacy Track. I am involved in several things on campus, with my favorites being NAACP and University of Miami Television. I am a firm believer in being the change I want to see, so with my future goals, I plan to come back and pour into my village. My future plans include being on television and being the Mayor of DC.

For me, 2020 was a year of growth because it forced

me to take time to explore new parts of myself. Some things that helped me to get through 2020 were my mentor, Camille, and having FaceTime calls with my friends from school. I hope that readers are able to go back and reflect on how far we have all come despite being shut down by a global pandemic.

My name is **Bilal Saleem** (he/him). I was 21 years old when I wrote my story, "Fire on My Doorstep." This is my second book  with Shout Mouse Press, as I am also a co-author of *I Am the Night Sky* (2019). I am currently a senior at the University of Maryland and am figuring out what's next. I'm excited to just take the world on, one day at a time — whether it be finding employment, learning something new, or working on another project with Shout Mouse, I'm here for it!

For me, 2020 was a journey in which I grew, adapted, learned about myself, and dealt with anything that stood in my way. It was a strange year for sure. To me, it felt like five years in one, but I wouldn't trade that growth for anything. Making playlists, experimenting in the kitchen, and late night FIFA sessions with some of my friends helped me get through it all. Most importantly, though, just talking to people helped me the most; it felt good to let everything out and leave the stress behind! I hope that, when reading this book, people take away the fact that life stops for nothing. Sometimes, life just happens and you can either let it get to you, or adapt and work through it. Despite all the nastiness and turmoil that the past couple of years had to offer, we're still getting through it, one day at a time. Be proud of yourself!

 My name is **Camal Shorter** (he/him). I was 19 when I wrote my story, "Born in Black." This is the second book that I've published with Shout Mouse Press. I am also a co-author of the children's book *Game of Pharaohs* (2019). I graduated from Coolidge High School, and did one year at Arizona State University. During my free time, I like to work and travel. In the future, I hope to get a job in the Marine Corps as an aviation mechanic and earn both my bachelor's and master's degrees.

For me, 2020 was a blessing in disguise because, surprisingly, at-home learning made it easier for me to focus on my school work. I got to end my junior and senior year of high school from home and my community service hours were waived. I hope our readers can be reminded to just keep trucking. 2020 taught me to focus on what I can control. I think oxygen can be a drug. If you can take five deep breaths every hour, your mood at least will be better. And a better mood is a better life lived.

My name is **Darne'Sha**
Walker (she/her). I was
22 when I wrote my story,
"Dear Al." I've co-authored
four other books with
Shout Mouse Press: *How to Grow Up like Me* (2014),
Princess of Fort Hill Shelter (2014), *Our Lives Matter* (2015),
and *Humans of Ballou* (2016). I graduated from Ballou
High School in 2017. I am currently working in a school
and in the future, I plan on becoming a youth counselor.

For me, 2020 was hard because I wasn't able to focus
on my health. I'm grateful for my nephew and sister who
helped me through the hard times. I hope that those who
read my story learn that it's okay to not be okay.

ABOUT THE ILLUSTRATORS

Alexis Williams (p. 30, p. 208) is a digital illustration artist based in Philadelphia. She was born in Montgomery, Alabama and raised by her grandparents in West Philadelphia. Her passion for the arts stemmed from childhood as she dealt with bullying and depression during her younger years. As she grew older, she discovered the world of anime, comic books, and cartoons, and began creating her own comic books in her spare time. After graduating from high school, Alexis attended Moore College of Art and Design, where she grew her passion for illustration, creating her very first published children's book. With the support of her family, friends, and professors, Alexis graduated with a BFA in Illustration and was awarded the William David Brown Award for Most Improved In Illustration. She is currently pursuing her dreams as an artist, creating unique and diverse digital art while at work on her second children's book.

Sade Adeshida (p. 88, p.272) is a self-taught illustrator and graphic designer from Nigeria. She is passionate about telling diverse African stories and recreating the same wonder and imagination she found in books as a kid. She has created illustrations for children's books and worked in character design and storyboarding for animation. Her driving passion will always be storytelling no matter the media, from design to books and animation. You can see more of her work at artoffolashade.com

Courtney Williams Skinner (p. 188, p. 238) is a digital artist based in Midlothian, Virginia. She is currently pursuing a Communication Arts degree at Virginia Commonwealth University. Her art is inspired by comics and animation, and she is driven to help bridge the gap in diverse stories. You can find her work at citriceart.myportfolio.com

Rae Flores (p. 4, p. 166) is an artist and writer based in Dallas-Fort Worth, Texas. She is a sophomore at the University of North Texas where she majors in Studio Art with a concentration in Drawing and Painting and minors in both English and Art History. She uses innovative illustration and fine art techniques alongside surrealist and fauvist concepts in order to create captivating visuals. Within her current work she is exploring the symbiotic relationship between nostalgia and art.

Vivian Jones (p. 58, p. 146) is an illustrator and designer currently based in Chicago with a BA in Illustration and Animation. Inspired by *Sailor Moon*, Vivian enjoys creating playful and colorful illustrations that invoke a whimsical feeling. "The sparkler the better," she says. Vivian enjoys using her work to elevate the voices of others and to tell stories that many can relate to. You can find her work at www.vivijon.com

ABOUT SHOUT MOUSE PRESS

Shout Mouse Press is a 501(c)3 nonprofit organization dedicated to centering and amplifying the voices of marginalized youth (ages 12+) via writing workshops, publication, and public speaking opportunities. The young people we coach are underrepresented — as characters and as creators — within young people's literature, and their perspectives underheard. Our work provides a platform for them to tell their own stories and, as published authors, to act as leaders and agents of change.

In collaboration with community-based partners, we have produced over 50 books by 500+ youth writers. Our authors are Black, Latinx, Muslim, immigrant, low-income, teen parents, incarcerated or formerly incarcerated, of other marginalized identities, and all the intersections therein from Greater Washington, DC. These authors change and reclaim the narrative, adding necessary complexity, empathy, and humanity to the stories of marginalized communities — and prove themselves as powerful thought leaders for all. There are currently over 100,000 Shout Mouse books in circulation across the country and around the world.

Learn more at **shoutmousepress.org**

OTHER YOUNG ADULT TITLES FROM SHOUT MOUSE PRESS

How to Grow Up like Me, Ballou Story Project (2014)

Trinitoga: Stories of Life in a Roughed-Up, Tough-Love, No-Good Hood, Beacon House (2014)

Our Lives Matter, Ballou Story Project (2015)

The Untold Story of the Real Me: Young Voices from Prison, Free Minds Book Club & Writing Workshop (2016)

Humans of Ballou, Ballou Story Project (2016)

The Day Tajon Got Shot, Beacon House (2017)

Voces Sin Fronteras: Our Stories, Our Truths, Latin American Youth Center (2018)

I Am the Night Sky: … & other reflections by Muslim American youth, Next Wave Muslim Initiative (2019)

The Ballou We Know, Ballou Story Project (2019)

They Called Me 299-359, Free Minds Book Club & Writing Workshop (2020)

When You Hear Me (You Hear Us), Free Minds Book Club & Writing Workshop (2021)

Black Boys Dreaming, Beacon House (2021)

For the full catalog of Shout Mouse books, including illustrated children's books, visit shoutmousepress.org.

For bulk orders, educator inquiries, and nonprofit discounts, contact orders@shoutmousepress.org.

Books are also available through Amazon.com, select bookstores, and select distributors, including Ingram, Baker & Taylor, and Follett.

CPSIA information can be obtained
at www.ICGtesting.com
Printed in the USA
LVHW071321140623
749737LV00003B/68